The Bulgarian Psychiatrist

Thomas McGonigle

Spuyten Duyvil

New York City

cover image: José Clemente Orozco. *The Subway* (1928)

Library of Congress Cataloging-in-Publication Data

Names: McGonigle, Thomas, author.
Title: The Bulgarian psychiatrist / Thomas Mcgonigle.
Description: New York City : Spuyten Duyvil, [2022]
Identifiers: LCCN 2022003621 | ISBN 9781956005554 (paperback)
Subjects: LCGFT: Novels.
Classification: LCC PS3563.C3644 B85 2022 | DDC 813/.54--dc23
LC record available at https://lccn.loc.gov/2022003621

There is no McGonigle but McGonigle, and McGonigle is his prophet... no, but seriously! McGonigle brings to *The Bulgarian Psychiatrist* the gifts of a born raconteur, a regression of digression that absorbs the reader toward the center of a hypnotic spiral of captivating prose.

Madison Smartt Bell

With a clear, historically informed gaze, *The Bulgarian Psychiatrist* examines an immigrant Bulgarian doctor in the US and the US within the immigrant, as narrated by its US author/narrator via free indirect discourse, interviews, photos, monologues, etc. That the book's primary pleasure is found in its looping run-ons and experimentation is understandable. After all, as the book says: "People can only take so much honesty. The fictions they live by are more powerful than anything they can say and which I can hear and it is this speaking and my listening." Especially recommended for readers of Laszlo Krasznahorkai and Gerhard Roth.

Tom Whalen

A truth stronger than fiction informs and shapes this double take of a fascinating case history, an intelligent, probing table-turning interrogation of the psychiatrist's loose tongued mental, emotional and spiritual condition. *The Bulgarian Psychiatrist* is a deft accomplishment worked by an able hand. McGonigle's trademark skill in adorned, head-on style is made manifest in this deep dive into the fathoms of human complexity.

James McCourt

Other books by Thomas McGonigle

In Patchogue
The Corpse Dream Of N. Petkov
Going to Patchogue
St. Patrick's Day: Another Day In Dublin

In Bulgarian

Диптих Преди Умиране
Diptych Before Dying
Предсмптните Биденир на Никола Петков
The Corpse Dream Of N. Petkov

To Trufana R., who first sheltered me in her house
on Ul, Yordan Lutibrodski in Nadeshda
and then at Vitosha Boulevard 53, Sofia...
took me to the Rila Monastery
and had me sit in Ivan Vasov's chair...
when such was allowed *back then* ...

George said he came to America with only a suitcase stuffed with neckties.

Yes, stuffed with neckties, he said, but couldn't begin to tell anyone how many ties were in the brown suitcase because both the number, three, seemed so insubstantial when it came to trying to see how three ties could fill up a suitcase and how could anyone who hadn't come to America with only one suitcase stuffed with ties, begin to understand how a suitcase—even a large brown fake leather suitcase from Bulgaria—could be stuffed with three neckties, two of which he never wore after he began to live in America, which is not to say he had ever worn those three neckties as he and his wife moved about the United States during the year and nine months before establishing themselves in Brooklyn, on the edge of Greenpoint, to be exact, a street over from McCarren Park—though there was a moment before that when they lived at another address in Brooklyn, in a street given over to as a topical description might: light industry, in a building stuffed, George later said, with Bulgarians and you can imagine what that was like, I am sure, stuffed with Bulgarians but we are not talking of that time...

No, he wore only one of the three ties as it was hard to unpack a suitcase stuffed with three ties and he was not trying to be thought philosophical because he and his wife had flown TWA from Frankfurt, that most factual of German cities, where they had been in residence immediately before receiving the notification that their application for a visa to the United States of America had been approved after having lived—for how many years had it been—in Hamburg where George was an attending psychiatrist in a clinic where fresh-cut flowers were placed in each patient's room reminding visitors of the complex glimmer of a possible recovery or funeral.

And it was not that he had always ever worn those three neckties in Germany or even before in Bulgaria. He was sure of having worn one of the ties and it was that tie he was wearing as he arrived in the United States of America and which appears around his neck and under the collar of the white shirt in the photograph his wife took of him as he walked down the steps from the plane.

Later, he learned that both actions: the walking down the steps from the plane and the picture taking were very rare actions, events almost, it could be said. Vera was standing on the runway, smelling the kerosene fuel he was sure, having paused, turning telling George STOP as he was about to continue his walking down the steps having been separated from Vera by a very large man and two women who had pushed their ways in front of George, who gave way as was his want.

Never again in all the times they were to come back from journeys abroad did any of these now three actions re-occur: the walking down the steps, the picture taking, the being separated by pushy large people.

There must have been some sort of renovation of the terminal going on and while they did not have to board a bus for a short ride to the ARRIVALS as they were familiar with in Sofia, George does not remember any obvious signs of construction but he was hardly looking out for it on this, his first arrival in The United States of America, wearing one of the three ties which he always said later filled up his suitcase.

Vera some time later must have had the snapshot enlarged into a framed 8x10 photograph. It was installed on the wall just before the bathroom door next to a drawing by Christo of an aspect of his plan to wrap the Reichstag in Berlin. One of the children had typed on a faded slip of lined school notebook paper: DAD'S ARRIVAL and inserted it in front of the glass but behind the wood of the lower right corner of the frame,

The tie, at the moment of the picture being taken, was blown by the wind up to George's right in the form of an abstract representation of the letter J in the Latin alphabet.

Indeed, it was this same narrow woven wool black tie which he constantly wore all those months as they traveled about in the United States and to be scrupulous, something George did not advocate, as it only led to the dreariest of consequences, though he was not making any real argument for lying, if someone might jump on his claim. There is however a difference between lying and being scrupulous and it might be supposed in some way he did not have three ties in his suitcase if he was wearing one of them both arriving and then while traveling in the country by train, plane, bus and rented, borrowed or private automobile.

George did not have an epiphany while traveling, as had Powys, in Houston. George was not given to any sort of religious enthusiasm. The very word *epiphany* frightened him because of its religious overtone and while he did not think very highly of the anti-religion campaigns by the communists in Bulgaria, there was still a residual materialist component to his life as a psychiatrist and now he did believe, if he could use that word, that there was really nothing much beyond the room in which he and his patient sat, right now, pretending of course all the while, there was something beyond the room, a dire necessity for many reasons: his patients were so lacking in imagination! If only they had imagination and the ability to forget! His patients were too often gripped by memories as tenacious as a terminal cancer and held by fantasies occasionally nailing them to the floor as in the famous joke much repeated with curious variations in the cafes in Sofia when he had been a medical student and still repeated to this day, Ilov told him only recently even with the fall of the communism now more than ten years ago.

George did wonder, when he thought about it so many years later, why Powys could use a word like *epiphany* when describing his discovery of the absence of sewers in Houston. Powys had ended up in that city while on his own journey around the United States, a journey which turned out to be both his first and final trip around the country. It was there in Houston Powys knew why he was moving to France with his family.

At the very least in France, Powys believed then, the French would not refuse to build a sewer system when there was only a need for one every three or four years, if even then, because how could a person look forward to living in a country, living out the years remaining, in a country where there was a city with many millions of people that could be built without a sewer.

However, when you arrive in a country with only a suitcase stuffed with neckties, you have only your own intelligence, George would say. You arrive with only what you have already put into your head. They could take everything away from you and they did that as far as they were able when you left a country like Bulgaria, back then, and it is hard to explain this, now, after the fall of the communism but then: you are suddenly in this country, in The United States of America, where you have to always remember you arrived with only a suitcase stuffed with neckties and you have to be always prepared to survive, once again, as you did then, as you stepped down from that plane—it was a TWA plane, an airline long gone from the skies and how it seemed then that TWA, Trans World Airways, along with PANAM, Pan American World Airlines, were symbols of the country George was coming to and this observation, one of so many, came back to him when he came to think about his curiosity about this Powys and his being able to decide on such a radical move as he had after his trip by railroad around the United States and from that moment in Houston as Powys tried to get across a main highway now under a foot of water because that was the year of the one flood every three years or was it four years and Powys wanted to get across the highway to have a drink which he needed and when he got back to St. Marks Place couldn't get it out of his mind that there were people in this country, in the United States of America, in a rich and powerful city of the United States of America who could make such a decision that prevented him on that day from getting across that highway to have a drink after a hard day... no, it was more like days which seemed like months of traveling on the so-called Amtrak where you didn't know what would break next, which part of the train would fall silent, dark, stop working and again Powys thought there had to be some better way to live and while he was prepared to think traveling by railroad was maybe not the best way to see America and he was prepared to make allowances for all the things that didn't work on the train he had learned to be tolerant, though that wasn't exactly the word he wanted, but anyway, he learned, somehow, as a grave digger for the Archdiocese of Brooklyn, when he was in the last years of high school, to overlook, to be prepared for nasty surprises, to the finding of things that they didn't expect to find when they went digging into these graves where surprisingly things move about which are not supposed to move about and really most of the time no one knew what was just a shovelful of earth away and later after both of the decisions were done into the past: when Powys had moved to France and when George and Vera had left Germany for The United States of America eventually finding themselves living in Brooklyn, Powys on a brief visit from Paris for the fortieth anniversary of his brother's ordination, asked George: did you think you would end up here in this bar on St. Marks Place—or where you are living in Brooklyn?—when you stepped down from that plane out there at Kennedy? and found yourself in a country where even the white people didn't have brains because by now I am sure you have discovered: white people in America are prepared to put up with the most awful situations if they think they are bound to get better—which of course they are not really—but there is no way to ever convince anyone in this country of that and you learn to be an American within an hour of landing in the United States of America, if not earlier as the world is full up of people who are destined to be Americans and are saturated with the idea: life is going to get better and better no matter what either the life or experience teaches them: isn't it a wonderful country where people in their eighties are thinking about, as they put it, career changes, though so much energy goes into not seeing what is going on as when I was on that train where at first the air conditioning broke and when that was fixed the toilets blocked up and then the kitchen no longer served food in the dining car and then they were able to serve hot food but the drinks could no longer be either heated or cooled while all the while the voice on the intercom was both apologizing for the temporary inconvenience and pointing out, you could now if you wanted, telephone loved ones from the special booth in the dining room and next year Amtrak was planning to introduce on-train shopping: it went on like this for the whole journey. Every train was being run into the ground and about the only thing you could say in its favor was for the most part the trains were empty except for these clumps of negroes and they were exactly that, clumps of negroes with fixed hair, from God knows where, going

God knows where and then old white couples: is there anything uglier than an old white couple who have a sporty look to themselves?: couples, mostly two women traveling together, having chopped off the balls of the dead husbands long before they were dead and now as the husbands were really dead the women were free to do, as they said, exactly what they wanted to do and Powys listened to the one couple, a man and a woman: the man was dressed in yellow and she had clipped off his balls—carrying them around in a sack and he had probably even forgotten she had done this—and the man had long ago forgotten he had ever had balls and both of them were pulling his and her carts along behind them on which oxygen bottles were strapped and they said together in almost one voice, they were on the way to some sort of special Olympics for older people not that we are that old   and Papa here has a lot of pep—and you get to compete to see who will not die this year and it could go on like all those days and yet it was in Houston when Powys tried to get across that highway, a highway that was probably not meant to be walked across in the first or second place—there are a lot of places like that in America: when you go out to the suburbs there are all those streets without sidewalks and that tells you how you are supposed to get around in a way that is not subtle at all, Powys told George in the bar on St. Marks Place in New York City and George heard it and George was thinking as he stepped down from the Trans World Airlines plane in New York City that day, *here I am*, as had so many people before me—he really did think those words to himself:

here I am, as so many of course before, I guess, he thought though wondering, a little, if they had consciously thought those words: *here I am* and there would be room enough for him and Vera, he was sure, it was a big country, The United States of America, and coming from a small country George knew very well what it was like to travel to a large country as when he went to Germany from Bulgaria and even earlier when he went to what was then called the Soviet Union—that was a big country, but in some way— he had to think about it more—the Soviet Union seemed to be a very small country even though he knew from the maps how large the Soviet Union was but it still felt like a tiny place and surely there would be room enough for their daughter who would be born in New York and would be an American: you can tell your teacher, George told his daughter in second grade upon the announcement of an ethnic festival to be held at the local elementary school: you do not have any ethnic foods, any ethnic costumes, because you are American even though your parents were born in Bulgaria, you are an American—even though your father arrived in this country with a suitcase stuffed with ties.

No, you don't have to tell her that and you are wondering why the teacher wants you to lie about what you are supposed to be when in fact she knows it as a fact that you were born here in New York City in Brooklyn Hospital and both of your parents were speaking English you are an American and if she wants to call me I would only be too happy to tell her this but I doubt she has the time or the inclination to call anyone who questions this sort of nonsense because it seems so strange anyone would question the idea of celebrating all the wonderful contributions... but Vera is saying George should remember their daughter is only in second grade and no second grade teacher wants to think about anything beyond getting through the day without having to listen to parents who want to remind her of the world beyond the teacher's desire to get home ahead of the traffic tie-ups on the LIE and of course plenty of room even for their son because it would be unfair to the daughter to be their only child, a one child who would have no society into which to be born but with a brother she would never be allowed to just think of herself, like so many only children, but maybe, George was saying, an only child spends all of its time thinking of being an only child so it has no time for thinking about how it will get on in the world while their daughter, with a brother now a year or so later, would have to think maybe a little about someone other than herself and George was getting ahead of himself by a long way and he still had to face the ordeal of going about The United States of America during their first year—at least not, as they say, *cap in hand* since he did not have a cap: hats, caps, berets, all such head coverings were a complicated business in Bulgaria and it all seemed so remote though he did notice the negroes of America had a great love for head coverings of all sorts and have always had the most peculiar desire to cover their heads though such a ramification would be a welcome respite from having to deal with people coming up to them, later, asking were they happy in New York? and hadn't they thought maybe it would have been better to have lived and been in other places in the United States of America before settling in New York City and George was trying to tell this to Powys who was still talking about the highway covered with water and how he was finally able to find a liquor store on the side of the highway where he was walking and he was lucky to get back to the train on time with his package from the package store because he didn't want to have to look for a hotel in Houston.

A few hours was enough time to see everything that was worth seeing in Houston and Powys did think it was fortunate the train was delayed for five hours in Houston for some reason though by then he no longer cared to know what was the source of the delay and he didn't have to be anywhere really on time. That was the best way to travel though he did find he was somehow absorbed by what other people were feeling about the delays and strange as it might seem some of the old people even thought they had to be someplace on time or their lives would have real problems though he did have to say it for the clumps of negroes: they just sat on their seats

like bumps on the logs they must have carried with them as a sort of Platonic resting spot because there was an art in the way they just waited, just sitting there and they did not complain, did not move a muscle of care but it could have been because we were Down South and they knew what was out there in Texas.

But what could be out there? as you say, in Texas that was not in every other state in The United States of America?

George was asking and I am sure you had to hide the bottle of liquor when you got back on the train. I noticed a young man once when we were flying somewhere in the United States of America who was drinking from his own bottle and suddenly this very large man was there pointing a gun at his head and demanding that he not do that anymore to which the young man asked if he was objecting to the humming or the way I get my mouth wet?

Vera and I were in the row behind this young man who I had not noticed for most of the flight as he was stretched out across four seats. The plane was pretty empty and this was back a long time ago just after we got here in as I said 1980 and I just didn't understand what it was all about and what the young man was really saying and the man put away his gun and went and sat in the row behind us. He had been drinking because I could smell the whiskey, I think it was on his breath, like he had been drinking all day and all night and he was there I guess to protect us, a man of the law, one of those, what do you call them, sky marshals?— we had read about sky marshals in Germany but the title seemed like something from a Karl May novel—people in America, I know, don't read Karl May novels but I had read them in Bulgaria and in Germany but not that he was really approved of in Bulgaria because he was disapproved of by all the communists who had read him years ago when they were learning German but I had that aunt who I once told you all about who was the reason why my father wanted me to learn German and she gave me a Karl May novel: yes, I do know they are trash but trash is still readable sometimes and I wanted to look at the museum that was somewhere in Germany but I never went there because that is too much like wondering why my father knew this woman and maybe it was part of the family romance a child has that she was my real mother and since my father never ever told me she was not my mother and I am sure I asked him who she was and now of course: how did this German woman come to live in Bulgaria and live in the street where I lived? But if I had not been there on the plane, I would not believe anyone who told me a story like this...

Well, I don't doubt you, Powys said. But many people would try to explain what happened to you and how you didn't understand and maybe you made a mistake or are you really sure you saw this man put a gun to the young man's head for humming and drinking from his own bottle on a plane flying or are you sure you aren't exaggerating or maybe you are making it up to make a point about something you think should have happened—where did you say you were flying from?

It was during that year before we settled down in Brooklyn and having to make money and once you start at making money you have to continue at making money but there is a moment before you start at making money when you worry about making money and you don't have a lot of money and we didn't have a lot of money but once you stop this short part of your life and then you are making some money and worrying about paying the Petes, as Americans like to say, *paying the Petes:* I used to make lists of idioms so I would know how people wanted me to talk... so you start making money and you are paying your Petes and you don't have the time anymore to just travel because all your time goes to making money in order to pay the Petes that making money forces you to do.

To settle down is one of those phrases that must have been on your list of idioms, Powys is saying. I don't know Bulgarian but I know you could not say something like that in Russian or in French. You are here now in the so-called New World and that is what people do in the New World: they settle it, settle down in it like a dog going round and round squashing the grass down making a nest into which to flop and then it sticks its nose up its rear-end to sleep, making the perfect circle, the perfect example of what Americans mean when they say they have settled down and are now making something of their lives: that constant remaining frustration because the back is not flexible enough to shove the nose as far up the arsehole, pardon my English, as they would really like and that is why Americans are a people that likes to move around a lot. They might think their shit smells sweet, as Edward once said, but they just can't get their noses as far up their own arseholes as they would like.

It's always possible, George is saying to Powys, now on St. Marks Place, but it must have still been dangerous to drink on the train from your own bottle unless you had one of those little rooms they have...

No, I didn't have a couchette. I thought I'd rough it and that was a mistake—another one of your idioms—it is hard enough to live with your wife's snoring but to listen to a car full of snoring people as it crosses the so-called Great Plains and you are thinking where are the Indians now that we really need them, armed with hand held missiles. Just put these people out of their miseries and no matter how much one drank the train just kept going on and on—I should have known better, I was always telling myself— and stopping for no reason at all though once in some spot the train stopped and this family was by the side of the train at a station that some senator forced the train to stick there for who knows why and this father was shaking his kid's hand and the kid was standing tall and looking like he was going off to take it like a man and get away from that awful place and find himself naturally in some other place that was even worse—it was all so moving: it would make you shit or throw up and so not able to make up my mind I just fell asleep thinking of a father shaking hands with a son he will never see again because the father will die in a car accident and the mother will get raped and strangled by some marauding Mexicans having a good time for the Cinco de Mayo and then they will burn the house down with all the other kids inside just for the hell of it because Spanish speaking people have a thing for fire.

I always told my brother, the priest there in Brooklyn, nothing disappeared in Brooklyn until the Puerto Ricans got there and then whole streets started to burn. The negroes like to squat. They don't like to burn—you can say that for the negro: they do not burn each other out while the Spanish have a thing for fire and for some reason, well, the Jews do too and it is no accident that in Brooklyn they talk about Jewish lightning—I wish I knew how to say it in Spanish as I am sure the Spanish give credit where credit is due and you know the joke about the two Jews who get together and are talking about business and one Jew talks about The Fire and losing all the stock that had just come in and other Jew is talking about the flood and all the stock that had just come in and the first Jew asks in a rare gesture of politeness, I can tell you, might I ask you a question: how do you cause a flood?

Growing up in Brooklyn you learn about these distinctions and no matter what they tell you—you know—they are true and the newspapers never ever are going to tell you the truth and no one will ever draw out any conclusion, in public, because if you do it in public the shit hits the fan and the resulting shit storm is of such giant proportions: everyone ends up covered in *merde* and while people like to play with shit they like to do it in the privacy of their own homes where they can let out their belts and really dig in, if you follow what I am getting at?

Maybe, George said wondering how he had gotten so far from that moment as he stepped down from the plane at JFK, as he was thinking, falling really, he should have said, off the plane and into this country that was to become his home or at the least the place where my children would be born and the place they could call home.

Where he came from didn't matter, really, he hoped, George would say sometimes and even now with Powys in front of him he wanted to say: yes, we do come from some place but what does it matter? you have only this moment in which you are sitting here in this bar talking with me and we are both accidents of what has happened to us and never is there any way of ever understanding, and don't think I can tell you what to understand means even in German as I could add letters and words to words building the precision for which the German language is known but it would still be unclear what anyone means when they say, *I understand what you are saying.*

Well... Powys is again on his train, his Amtrak train, as it made for New Orleans—no, not his train: the train he was riding on, in, with—while he is thinking and not happy to just be thinking, he thinks, the negroes are growing agitated. They are back in the promised land of their ancestors stirred with the thoughts that got them out of this place to the streets of Chicago and New York: you know the negroes of Louisiana ended up in Chicago and we got the negroes from North Carolina in Brooklyn: isn't it wonderful when you hear a negro in New York going on about home to North Carolina so full of pride of where they come from, back home down there, as they like to say— not like here in Brooklyn—you can leave your back door open and no one is going to walk in and strip the house bare but even in North Carolina, they slyly admit, things are changing and are not the way they used to be and it has something to do with all those people from Up North moving down here bringing with them... and I am thinking, Powys is saying, of the forgetfulness involved, more so than in any Irish person though no one has ever measured the ability of the Irish to either remember or forget though it is said the Irish never forget or learn anything from what they have remembered, so what's the point? but that is to expect too much of any people: no one really learns anything from history or from what is remembered, just words repeated over and over again becoming a glob of tasteless bubble gum you can't even stick under the desk.

While Powys was sitting on the train measuring heads, it could well have been—like that Greenwich Village character who wrote a story for Ezra Pound about being sent out to North Dakota to measure heads of Indians for Harvard University—but all that was before all of your times, Powys says quickly, I mean, the Greenwich Village stuff which I only saw the end of before the tourists and the kids set up permanent homes on the streets of the Village repeating that old song: the Village was a'changing while the only people who ever referred to Greenwich Village were—God, who knows?—and there was no room in the inn for any of us   and while it would be easy to steal everyone's present by going on and on about the good old days there were still some characters left about in the Village, when I got here and had those rooms over on First Avenue.

One of those guys was drunk most of the time and he was always talking about measuring the heads of Indians with that other drunk who got himself killed by some sort of drifter back in the summer of love or what passed for it in New York City: boy, that was a brief season... Bergen told me this, I didn't know him myself but sitting on the train I thought it might have been interesting to get out the measuring tape and start measuring the heads of the negroes and see if Harvard University might be interested in some primary research... like when that man Carleton Coon was at Harvard—you can't make up names like that—sending out young men to measure the heads of Indians in North Dakota.

They don't measure heads anymore, George is saying, even in Bulgaria where the communists held on to certain theories of development of the new man, the new Socialist man who was going to run the world if only they could get the social system exactly established and then the brain would follow and you would have men who would walk naturally with chin on high, eyes looking to the future, hearts beating to a drummer that never let up the beat of the necessary production goals for whatever month we are talking about.

But in The United States of America I have noticed people talked about other sorts of the future and I could never figure out the American sense of time and still can't figure it out. Little children here I notice were already in mourning for what they had experienced in their childhoods, they told me, when I tried to talk to these children when I went to pick up Nikolas from his school. These little children, maybe eight or nine years old, and were already talking as if half their lives had been lived and they were wondering what had happened to the years gone by: of course I had to get used to the rituals of American life, as they told us to call them: how children graduate, is that the word, from their pre-kindergarten class and then they graduate from their kindergarten and then they are ready to enter first grade and they graduate from that class and then there is a little break and by then what can come along: everything is commemorated—even in the sports club Nikolas joined, because his mother thought he should, there was a graduation ceremony of some sort and that was made a big deal of and you wonder when something really big comes along and there is no celebration for it—has it really happened?

Maybe I should have read American poetry or something but I don't like poetry and people are always giving me poetry books to read. I can never really read it because I think you have to read poetry in your mother language as that is the only poetry you can really understand.

In Bulgaria there was no poetry coming from my mother and of course I had two mothers as I told you or thought I did have two mothers which is the same as having two mothers which can complicate a life but my father did not allow it to be complicated. Instead, my father, he provided shadows and shade into which I could find my own life and when I went to Sofia I did not think of these things— even at the Medical Academy—and when I came to The United States of America I had other things to think about which was a good thing and soon enough after Vera and I traveled about in The United States of America we had too many things to wonder and worry about that there was no time to think again and again about my two mothers or the thought I might have two mothers—but that is more a strange sort of poetry wanting to take up a place within my memory because for the longest time nothing much happens in my life until I too took a little journey in these United States of the Americans but I didn't go to Texas, to Houston, Texas, like Powys did but to Washington for a conference on what I had been thinking about and what I talked about in Bulgaria after I went back there after the fall of the communism—but all of that is far in the future from the moment when walking down the steps from the plane at JFK and all of The United States of America was before our steps, you could say if you chose to, I suppose, though there was just a little hint of that, I guess, but in the afternoon as we made our way to the customs and before, the passport office where they were to look at our papers surely as if we were criminals, I thought, as we walked through curving corridor after corridor—of course we were criminals: that is the point of such a suspense   before the presentation of our passports—with all the people from the plane, and at each bend of the corridor large uniformed men who were always smiling for some reason and then halted where we were separated from returning citizens of The United States of America and being told, one by one to go to this sort of booth where I placed my passport on the counter but suddenly this officer looked up, from what he was reading, looking at my picture and then he walked out of his booth and I thought something truly had gone wrong and he reached out and I understood I was to shake his hand and he was saying, *Welcome to The United States of America.*

As quickly as the officer walked out of the booth he

had returned to the booth and was pushing my passport back across the counter and was turning to the next person coming along behind me. I was looking for Vera who was stuck behind this... I forget who it might be and eventually she came along, though no one had welcomed her with a handshake and she didn't really believe me and it must have been a mistake, she was saying, as we went to look for the luggage: my suitcase with the ties as I said.

I again told Vera of the officer who shook my hand with no explanation and she couldn't believe it had happened to me, though she thought she saw him do it and she thought it was probably a way they had to make sure I was of the right height as it stated in the passport and also it was a way to really intimidate people when they came to The United States of America: what better way to do this than to shake your hand but I had to tell her I didn't think it was like she was saying—maybe the officer really did feel like welcoming me to The United States of America and there are some things you can't explain and any way it had happened and it was just one of those things, sometimes, that happen to you which maybe means something and maybe does not mean something though in this case I thought it interesting that Vera suddenly became suspicious and sounded like sentences from a newspaper in Sofia where a journalist would describe how hard it was to come to The United States of America and how Americans didn't really want anyone to come to their country and they were always suspicious of people who came from the Socialist Countries because we were bringing our ideals of how there was a better way to live and no American was eager to talk and be with people from our country because of the fear of the police and all the questions that would have to be endured if such a conversation was held.

Of course such articles were rare because they reminded people that they were not able to travel to find out for themselves what it was like to arrive in The United States of America.

Vera understood it was maybe foolish on her part but George was never ever really sure of knowing this and allowed it to pass as they gathered their suitcases: well, George gathered his suitcase and together they found themselves before another man who just looked at the form they had filled out: they declared they were not bringing any animal or plant materials, had no gifts for friends or family, had not bought anything while abroad.

The form stamped and they were waved ever so slightly with a sweep of hand to the exit.

Dutifully they found the Carey bus into the city as a German colleague of George's has instructed them to do and when they were deposited on the street perpendicular to the front of Grand Central Station they were told to walk two or was it three avenues to the west and found themselves in a large hotel which is no longer there now in the present of this writing. They had been warned that the hotel was not as bad as it looked and they would surely find it interesting as a place to look back upon when they were more established in The United States of America. It would be a good place to begin the stay in the country because you will see all the different sorts of people who make up the country and there will be many people from Europe also in the hotel—the sort who are looking for the authentic American hotel—so it will be a transition and you will see there are some people who live in the hotel and you can shop with them in the store next to the hotel where you can buy all the things you will need and you will not have to eat in the restaurant in the hotel which will not be appealing to you and might even remind you of Bulgaria, though this friend who said it was as sure as George would be after he looked into the restaurant on the second day of their stay. It was a very large room with a very high ceiling and tables seemed to hug the floor and everyone for some reason was huddled over their food not looking up even as the waiter placed or removed plates or when there might be a sudden scream from one of the many corners, it seemed, of the room… no one looked up because to look up was to be engaged and possibly… George was sure of this from his reading and his experience in the hospitals in both Germany and in Bulgaria: if you look in the direction of a scream you will eventually or suddenly become caught up in the life of the screamer and there is no escaping then because the look will fasten on the person replying even with only a look and no matter what you later do it was the wrong step to have taken.

So, George well understood why no one looked up when a scream went out from one of the corners and no one answered it though by holding his napkin to the side of his head as if scratching his earlobe he saw that the loud scream, belonged to a tiny well-dressed woman who was sitting by herself at a round table and on each of the three chairs about the table she had placed a yellow chicken doll that he had noticed a man selling on Times Square last night and which it seemed ugly fat girls demanded from their boyfriends as part of the down payment for what might happen later in the evening. These chicken dolls, the size of a child, were covered with rows of filmy cloth to represent feathers and the chicken's beak was bright orange and its mouth open in an appalling gesture of affection. The eyes were of a startling blue and a tiny tear was represented as falling from each of these characteristics.

The woman was at lunch with three of these objects and George, you might say, as he did to himself: surely this woman might be thought eccentric and it would all be too easy to caricature The United States of America through her as a lonely place where people were so desperate for companionship that they... but no reflection was really possible, he had to admit, when it came to the mad: he noted this woman, went back to the possibility of staying in the restaurant but decided that he could wait to dine later.

George would remember the woman but refuse to limit his memory to such an example. The world is packed with the mad, with all those we would not want to live with though in so many cases we were already living with them and choosing not to really see who they were. If we look too closely, if we discriminate with too much scrupulosity among those who we come into contact with, if we as they say in the villages: keep pulling up the roses to see if they are doing well you end up with a fist full of dead weeds to be stuffed into your own mouth when they dump you into your final hole.

George went exploring—self-consciously even saying: let's explore the streets—with Vera in those first days in New York. The movies in Germany, he had to admit, had prepared him a little for his walking about the streets. He knew not to look up at the skyscrapers (he did call them that, rather than saying the tall buildings—skyscraper seemed a word you read but never spoke) and not to always be wondering about how straight the streets and avenues were and how quickly people walked, how everyone walked with an air of knowing where they were going.

However, he was not prepared for the silence of the New York streets. Never did he hear human voices. He noted this as a fact and either it meant something or it was a something for further investigation.

He did not like the process—even then before the years had convinced him of the truth of it—by which an experience could be turned into a word like epiphany, that same word that Powys had used so freely. The very word epiphany frightened George a little because of its religious over-tone and while he did not think very highly of the anti-religion campaigns of the communists in Bulgaria and his own children would be baptized into the Bulgarian Orthodox Church when that time came, there is still a deep—he was aware of it—anti-religious component to his life as a psychiatrist and now he did believe there was really nothing much beyond the room in which he and the patient sat, pretending of course, there was something beyond the room which was necessary for so many reasons.

His patients were so lacking in imagination or they had imaginations so totally un-connected to any sense of what George for lack of words, thankfully, simply described as being in the real world without worrying about how to go about defining any of those words: the real world—if only his patients had the ability to forget: wasn't that the first hallmark of a genuine imagination... to forget and then invent... so gripped they were by in-action or often action so frantic as to be a sort of in-action wearing away the earth from under their moving feet, down so deep, they could be said to be digging their own graves.

—PAUSE—

But George is demanding more attention and Caphart is nudging himself into the tale and wants to get on with the lash across the backs of those recalcitrant obstreperous sacks of work who thought they could escape their fate* and George is saying the lash never leaves the world ——————— and even in the camp in Bulgaria the superintendent would initiate his son into the routine and place him in such a way that his coat would be speckled with the clubbed flung blood...

To have a grown son who for years had been going on about how I had abandoned him to his mother who did not want to be a mother, who so quickly tired of the tedium yet somehow she had raised him as best she could with no help from you which even if it was her addled decision to keep me in the world should have demanded of you some sort of human response.

Nothing is what he got and nothing I gave.

That is one version but no worse than my telling the mother of two children…

—is this foreshadowing or personal indulgence of a voice wanting to be heard—

Quickly, George was a book buyer. I would see him sometimes after he had come from The Strand with a new edition of the stories of Tolstoy or a classic history of Rome or a complete Shakespeare that was actually well printed and readable: he bought these for his children and while I do not know if they will ever read them I have bought them and they are on the shelf. That is what a father is supposed to do even if he knows they will never read the books. I didn't read the books my father had bought for me. That did not prevent me from buying books for the children.

The books would be on the table in the kitchen until Vera came home if George had returned early that day from his patients. She would notice the little pile of books when she came home, why have *you* bought even more books for the children who have no interest in them and have never opened a single one of them. You pile them on the shelf and I noticed you bought a second copy of *The Three Musketeers* as if a second copy would have a different effect on…

George did not argue. There was nothing to be said and

while he knew, silence is the most awful weapon, there were times when he simply did not know what to say and even after listening for so many years and this is what people found strange: he did not remember what people said. He was not supposed to remember what people said. That is what fiction writers do and then do something with those memories. His patients said things and the saying was in their own interests. If he missed something, he knew, from all the years, whatever it was would be said again and if for some tiny reason it was not said again it was of no importance.

People repeated themselves. They certainly did not realize how frequently they repeated themselves.

However George resisted as well as he was able the temptation to give into totally forgetting what people said. He did know what people were saying and while he did not keep notes, and that was a failure on his part, a Balkan sort of laziness, he might even say—it was not a Turkish form of laziness.

Powerful people were always forgetting things. The powerless forgot and forgot and then were suddenly beaten over the head by what they had forgotten and turned on their tormentor with great claims to having remembered every single slight, every slip of the tongue, twist of the blade.

The children had their busy lives and he would not insist upon the books. The books would be available and just this availability seemed such a pathetic reason he used it only once and Vera looked at him with that look—how well he knew it—reminding him, she was the one who made the bigger income in spite of having no education.

PAUSE

George wanted to see me at the Grass Roots. On Tuesday not like the usual Wednesday. He had called, was I planning to be there on Wednesday? Are you sure you will be there? Can you be there on Tuesday? Will the others be there? I have something to ask you, both.

Being of sound mind. I qualify, do you think?

Here, right now in the Grass Roots?

Never did George ask questions he didn't have the answers for. He was polite in that way. To ask a question was to show either some sort of respect or just simple trust. He would never ask a question with no possibility of an answer. What is the point of asking such questions?

Why do children die?

The perfect way to end the possibility of talking.

What is going to happen?

I am going into the hospital. They are going to replace my heart valves with pig valves. A routine operation, the doctor says. For you I said and the doctor said yes for me and you know the consequences and the risks and what will happen if we don't do the operation and I told the doctor I knew what would happen if he did the operation and I know what will happen eventually to me, of course, and he said that is for everyone and you are no different except you know it more clearly.

I can die right now or right then on the operating table or after the operation or in three weeks or in eight months or in ten years…

Like everyone, the doctor said.

Except I am the one who is going to be opened up.

That is true.

The operation didn't kill George.

PAUSE

Pages of …

It is the futility, George was saying, a patient comes to me and tells me his story, no, that is not exactly right because it is better to say, a patient comes to me and tells me and tells me.

I listen to him and it is in what I can not tell him there is the possibility of his life.

Think, George says, if I had said, a patient comes to me and tells me his story and tells me his story again and again or he tells me again and again his story.

Of course it is obvious, is it not obvious? a patient tells the story and he tells his story over and over again for years in the most ideal circumstances.

(You have heard this, George says with his two hands in front of him as if forming a parenthesis, all your life. It's so common that: to suggest otherwise is to be thought obvious and stupid and even patients will perform so faithfully their assigned role)

Naturally, George would pause, drink from the Scotch in front of him, finding it empty puts the glass down on the bar top and with a shy sort of gesture involving the slightest movement of the second finger of his right hand begins to try to catch the easily distracted eyes of Bobby and while it is not possible as in the 55 Bar in desperation to call from the payphone in the back to the phone behind the bar in order to speed the movement of bartender from one end of the bar to the other...

It is the futility, George is saying, again to me, a patient brings to me what he thinks is his story and it is in the telling of it—

However, can I say that? he has to come to realize if it is only a story there is probably no hope for him, the futility of the story—the storying of his life is such a powerful and ever thickening shell encasing him in the miserable situation that has found him:

but at least it is his story, but at least it is his story, his sole possession: he is adamant in this—this man has in his possession all that the world has to offer otherwise he would not be able to afford to come to see me.

I have never had a patient who has ever missed a meal in his life even if he is dressed in rags or verbally proclaims his poverty or a financial situation becoming impossible: how they do like to say that all too often as they write out the check or say that the check will be coming from a parent, a lawyer—and I listen, I listen and if I ever indicate any of this, I might as well shove him into a hole in the ground, off a tall building, cut his throat, wrist.

Occasionally a crack might develop in the story so, the tiniest sliver of hope appears…

Oh, please don't remind me of how contaminated hope has become: a steel jaw in *Svabodna* Park pointed to the sky.

⸻➤↑

The symptoms of sickness, wrote Kalb, must be considered as works of art. *The Will to Sickness*, Gerhard Roth

He is talking. The windshield had been covered with frost. Remember it was January after all. I am not sure I will miss the…

It's a straight shot across the Air Force base. The emptiness does not mirror what is inside, really. They say it does for some people but not for me. I like the looking into emptiness though it sounds pretentious I know the desert is not empty, far from it.

His name had almost, just almost, become clear so we could all follow who is talking—you know—the guy from the Marine Motel, seems all a little too arch as in a recent formulation: *destroyed them from the earth.*

But George intrudes, again:

I have never cured anyone.

Finally, able to say it now: the pig valve is in my body—do you know what it feels like to have a thing inside you?

To know, really know that all of your real body is not…

The mystery of women of course—it is not a foreign thing. Homosexuals are always taking things into their bodies. That is why they are abnormal, Freud might say. Women are made for the taking of things inside their bodies.

George has been drinking again and I have been listening to him in The Grass Roots. One of those nights when no one we knew came in.

It had been a long day with my patients. I am old fashioned. They become part of my life even though I have them out there as I am supposed to. But how to remain human, isn't that all anyone can ask for...

Once one of them, you know who I mean, became human for a moment and said to me, very quickly as we walked near *Sveta Nedelya*: just leave, or maybe it would be better to catch it exactly: just go away, he said.

This man didn't have to say anything more. It was all he was capable of. I had helped him with his son who was very sick. I won't tell you who he was. It doesn't matter but I knew that he was speaking for them. I had helped some of them when they had no one else to turn to: for some reason they understood that nothing else worked.

George is talking about Bulgaria, a Bulgaria that no longer exists and even then it did not exist or at least people did not see it or even know it might exist.

I am still sometimes in Bulgaria. You cannot take a language out of the brain. A new language does not replace the old language. Bulgaria under the communism: people look at me when I say that: none of that exists except in books.

But in my head, I want to say and I know they are holding back from saying: poor man.

I should tell you—like I told George—about going into **The Guardian** office in London having come back from Sofia and trying to talk about the Freedom Village that was set up in front of the Communist Party building in the summer of 1990. I did not know how to make it vivid to these English people. They had a man in Bulgaria. They did not want another voice. One voice was enough and he had his two or three inches somewhere in the paper. No one that summer, that hottest summer on record in England, wanted to know about a Freedom Village in Bulgaria. It sounded like an American resort filled with people waving Bibles and shotguns, Clare told me and everybody in England knew enough about Bulgaria. I had known Clare for twenty years. That didn't help. At all. She thought I was making it up and I wasn't trained to look at things like their man in Bulgaria.

And George embarrassed me by saying, you understand this Bulgaria, all these Bulgarias, without speaking the language. You are as powerless as all this implies and is understood. No one in the West will care what you have to say. No one in Bulgaria will understand what you are saying.

If they find you still in Bulgaria, this man was telling me, you would be sent to the psychotic ward, George was saying. That is how I was to understand this man's words: just go away.   I understood what they meant: just go away. They didn't need to say anything more. If I did not understand what they were saying they had a place for me in one of their hospitals...

To try to understand driving across the Air Force range—I should have looked carefully at the map, the Barry M. Goldwater Air Force Range—with a road like a wire bisecting it on the way to Barstow—this time—and George nudging aside the man in Ajo who I see walking into a diner in a small strip mall just outside...

though George is going to talk about violent death also: torture, beatings, and how a man put on a dead man's clothes as if he always belonged in that clothing: without the slightest twinge of guilt: something that is not in his or their vocabulary... but this man in Ajo... where has he gotten to?

Can I pretend I knocked on the door where he was staying or can I write, his car was not there in the morning? Probably on his way up to Phoenix and then to get the lead out as he had to be in Chloride before it got dark. His wife was waiting for him and the child was going to need a lot of love, and he would curl his lip as if anyone knew what the phrase: *she will need a lot of love.*

Forget the local colour, George is saying. You are not some guy stuck in a pig hole in the countryside. I want you to move me about in your mind. I want not to be fixed like some dead bug tacked to an exhibit wall. I was happy, every day I was happy to see the new buildings going up in New York—do you remember where we lived in Brooklyn? None of it is there anymore. The landlord moved to Florida. The building was torn down and no one knows what it looked like. That is not something to mourn, at all. A person can always go to Paris to see things that stay the way they were. Every city is different. People get confused when they try to criticize a city with the standards of another city. It is a way to go crazy. You have to see what is in front of your face, first. You go crazy if you can not look and see what is really there... never forget that.

So throw in the picture from that cemetery. A moment before the plastic flowers get blown apart to become burial rubbish against the barbed wire fence. Make sure you mention the birthday candles arranged in the earth but not lit. To be lit by lightning, you can suppose…memorial rubbish for someone going to a shop, buying, carrying, leaving behind, blown away… idle sentimentality, poor man.

You told me once of walking around in Dublin and wanting to almost cry because it was all so painful… to have admitted that is sufficient. No one walks around in New York talking: do you remember when… the city is a wonderful drug wiping itself clear and wipes away those thoughts from the people who find themselves living here. And it's something to be proud of, not scorned like some pretend. When I go Upstate Vera's sister has a photo book of OLDE NEW YORK. She bought it because she thought she would impress me with her new found interest in history. I wanted to tell her what Ed said in the Grass Roots: Francis Bacon liked old photographs of masses of people because all the people in the photographs were dead, now, and I am alive looking at them.

⸺↑

While George did not know the novels of Gerhard Roth—it is a permanent regret we were not able to talk about them—George did tell me he had read two books by Max Frisch: *Man in the Holocene* and *I'm not Stiller.*

He did not want to forget his German. While no longer having a desire to go to Germany the language allowed him to think, he said. Only if you know German could you know what I am trying to say. It is not that German is better than English but English is the language of the streets, of this bar, of the television, the language my patients speak to me, the language my children use and which I talk to them in. German is my other language. The language took me out of Bulgaria even during the Communism. I have told you all of that and even in East Germany the language, though damaged by the communism, could not have been hurt at its center which even resisted the Nazis contrary to what some would have you believe. People do not lose everything and yet rebuilt everything if there is nothing at the center. That is a mystery, George would say. I wonder if everything was wiped out in the United States if it could all be re-built. To think of the United States broken into pieces and then divided into two competing systems and then re-united! Americans do not know what it means to lose. Bulgarians only know about loss and it is nothing to be proud of, nothing is gained from the experience. Germany is different, in some way, and it drives some people crazy but they can't do anything about it.

Frisch is not German and so his German is not really German—it is something else to be sure and I am not qualified to tell you how this is. A patient told me about his books. He said I might be interested in them. I am interested in them but they are not... he is not Thomas Mann and while *Doctor Faustus* is no longer the book I read in Germany when I at first had the night duty. It is a blackening book that allows you to think something is going to be there in the daylight though gradually you begin to realize you don't have time enough to listen, to think, to seek out what Mann wants you to seek out. That is why I insisted on going to the Heiner Goebbels concert in Brooklyn. None of it made sense but it was a going out into something that maybe did not make sense and sometimes that is just fine and maybe even good.

···→↑

...to avoid falling into the machinery of facts.

On the Brink. Gerhard Roth

George did not take notes when he listened to his patients.

Why should I?

I am not taking notes at a lecture.

I am not preparing for an examination.

I do not have to have notes for a debate.

I do not have to remember everything that is said.

I am not making a list to make a point.

If the patient sees me writing something down he is wondering what I am writing down and wants to know what I have written down as if that could be the secret he's been looking for and no matter what I tell him and I cannot tell him the truth: I was only writing down what I had to get from the store on the way home after this session…

The insurance wants some sort of notes but they don't want too much. No one wants too much detail, but patients always say they want their own details taken seriously.

I have no need to remember every single thing said.

That is the job of the patient.

They remember each and every thing.

It is their basic problem.

They remember everything to no purpose.

They repeat the details.

Over and over again.

A forgotten detail could destroy the life.

A forgotten detail could end the life.

They are always hoping to find a detail they have forgotten.

And something else always happens.

What did this dream mean?

I turn the question back and they resent this.

But not always.

A fist breaking through a car window is something to be afraid of.

I see their lips moving over the word *afraid*.

I do talk with them sometimes though they are not able to listen to what they have not been prepared to hear.

↑ ↳

The pen writes the words…or the words prepare the pen.

Am I to remember such phrases that patients use when they begin to tell me of some dream I have forgotten before they get to the end of their telling.

Even they have difficulty getting to the end of the dream because they really do not want me to tell them what it means.

They know what it means.

If they are almost honest with themselves they begin to say this and I know I will not be seeing this patient for many more sessions.

People can only take so much honesty. The fictions they live by are more powerful than anything they can say and which I can hear and it is this speaking and my listening…

Do not ask me what I am supposed to hear.

If the patient does not begin to listen to himself there is no point to any of this.

There is the question of money but no one objects to paying though they would like someone else to pay.

No one has ever tried to negotiate with me about money.

Though money is almost always somewhere in the story or the fiction we are working our way through.

By having the office in Soho I am surrounded by art… well that was once upon a time.

Now it is no longer the case but the landlord can't think of what to put into my space here in his basement.

I would like to have patients who could pay more.

What I charge is too low and people think there is something wrong with me because they are paying what they are paying.

I like the office being on Sullivan Street.

Vera has her work on the Upper East Side.

I am not saying one is better than the other.

If you mention something like that people think you are criticizing something which they really can't put their clumsy fingers on.

You can never mention distinctions because always: is one better than the other?

It has happened: the voice of a patient enters my head and I begin to think as that person must have thought or not thought when he was speaking. I have not become the voice of a woman so I have not become insane, yet.

⋯→↑

George would walk down to his office from an institute on University Place where he also saw patients. He had no control over the patients at The Institute. They walked in off the street and if there was an opening in his schedule he was assigned to them. They came and went with their problems and issues—George did not like the word *issue* but it was used more and more—and the patient would try him out for a session or two and then usually move on. He was paid for the patients who stayed beyond a trial session.

The trial sessions were on my cuff, he would say. The patient was in control in a way that did not bode well for either of us.

Where is your accent from?

Does it matter? I wanted to reply but that only lead to even more difficult questions.

Or imagine, George says on another night in The Grass Roots: A patient walks in with her or his name on a piece of paper and my name with the number of my cubicle filled in by the receptionist. What do I ask? Do I wait for the patient to say something?

The air conditioned noise and I am… they just start in: Malcolm said I was a piece of shit and he was tired of eating shit every day of the week and what was he supposed to do now that he no longer had the taste for the shit and I am thinking for too long I have kissed that mouth filled with rotting teeth and how could anything come out of such a mouth and why had I kissed it all these years with the feeling of gagging yet unable to vomit, unable to vomit in the way I wanted but what if he thought I was offering him something I could no longer control as I was offered up to him by my mother who likes him very much and was happy I had met a real man after all the losers you have dragged home to meet me.

But I didn't tell you this of course, George is saying, you imagined it for me and I listen to what you think I hear as if I hear anything as clear as what you can imagine.

George lived in an apartment off Patriarh Evtimii that January when I went to visit him from London.[1]

Of course I am driving away from Ajo on my way to Barstow. That's the plan. George and I would go walking around in Sofia. It had both changed and remained the same. How fortunate George would be saying to me: going to a place where you have no memories so you can drag along anything you want. You don't have to endlessly compare the present with the fragments of the past that get called back no matter if we want them or not.

In Sofia, as in Dublin, as in Istanbul, as in Paris, as in Helsinki, as in Patchogue and so for George when he went back to Pleven to visit with his brother and their mother… how quickly one is again the son walking through a version of the family romance.

Of course you know why I am in New York and it does not matter where I live in New York. No place in the city resonates in any way for me. It is just New York City: an impossible place, now where I live, where my children were born. For you it is different. I go down to the courts with no fear, I go to the hospital with no fear, I walk past where we lived in Brooklyn… I walk to the apartment in Forest Hills. I do not tell myself I wish I was back in Brooklyn.

---

1 You did not miss something. Eventually you will read about this visit to Sofia. The subject here is George not my visit to Sofia.

Would I wish to see Medy, to see those Bulgarians, that Russian woman who was dying for too long, though for some reason you thought her exotic, even Bulgarian, confusing the story Lydia told you about another Bulgarian woman in Nadeshda who had had many lovers and was now just waiting, waiting like a character in a novel. But I am sure you have forgotten more about her life as you only had a few sentences from Lydia about this woman and you think I had wanted to be back in Pleven:

George went to Pleven because a son must go to where his mother is, where his brother is. It is where I came from, before I went to Sofia.

Once Lydia got Medy away from Brooklyn she did not go back there to see where her mother had lived. Lydia was a good American with all the old address books thrown away, all the old letters torn up, the photographs edited with scissors. She is where she always wanted to be: away from you—because all you could talk about is I left the train at five o'clock in the afternoon…

It is not a suggestion for keeping a friend if you are always replanting the memory of your first meeting. Plants like people can not take it. They both wilt… which is an awful way to describe a human being—a human being is not a plant, a shrub, a weed or flower, let alone a tree or blade of grass.

Avoided it long enough. Sitting in the car in Desert Center. The air conditioner is working. The windows should be opened and the heat allowed to come in. Get the feel of the place. Hear a truck down shifting as it turns off the interstate.

Does the photo do justice to the place? Had you to be there to have some sort of feeling?

George was talking about a soldier who during his basic training was assigned the job of listening to what his fellow soldiers talked about in their sleep. While George thought this might be a made up story—fantastic to be sure—but given a certain desire on the part of the young man, now old and wanting to give a gift to this visitor—George was assured that one soldier was arrested for talking in his sleep about how difficult it had been to get across the border into Italy after the journey across Yugoslavia.

George was talking about going to the apartment of this powerful man. You know what I am talking about, the sort of man and the fear and respect people have for certain men. The man who would warn me to leave. You had been with Medy to see that man who was a director of the police in Sofia. You were embarrassed when Medy kissed the backs of his hands. You had never seen her do something like that. The way she clutched at them and sounds of the kissing or the way the man held his hands there in front of him not telling her it was enough it was enough—no, he just had them out here and then he abruptly pulled them away... the harshness of the gesture...

Medy was a woman from the country and had lived in Sofia for many many years and yet she had gone back, in that powerful man's apartment to a moment she must have seen in her childhood… you on the other hand noticed the glass fronted bookshelves with the complete editions of Tolstoy and Dostoevsky in Russian, none of which this man had read, Lydia would say as he could barely read and write in Bulgarian but those books were there because they were what he thought a person of his position and now living in Sofia was supposed to have in his apartment and you must never forget the reason we had been to see him: Medy's mother had been nice to the boy after his parents had been killed back in the village, killed because of politics in the 1930s but Medy's mother had been nice to the boy because he was a boy now alone whose mother and father had been murdered and that is what a person is supposed to do but it had taken Medy a long time to remember this boy and then hearing who he had become and the difficulty of getting to see him and…so much money had to be spent on the way to getting to see the man and the conversation in the apartment had been very very brief because there was nothing to be said: a question after the mention of the name of the town *Strashitza* and this man still took the money to help him with his memory of when he was a boy—money he hardly needed as he was beyond needing money as all the people who were like him did not live in an economy that used money in the sense you and I would use that word but it was because of him Lydia would have a Bulgarian passport with only three numbers… that's how rare they were, a nice red leather covered passport…

But George was talking about visiting a man he knew to be a very powerful man who was now living in the apartment of another man who had been executed as an enemy of the people. The man had just moved into the man's apartment and inhabited his possessions. He had been supplied with two people who kept the apartment cleaned. He did not feel capable of keeping it clean. The furniture and rugs, the pictures on the walls, the glass chandelier had all come from abroad, from The West.

George noticed this man walked about in the apartment as if it was a museum though he told George all these things had been in his family for a hundred years but George knew the man had moved to Sofia just after or just before 9 September. The man did not allow his hand to graze the tops of the chairs. He patted them as if he was tamping them down into the earth or tamping something else down into the earth but that would be a psychological crudity if I said this in New York but in Sofia people were like this and remember when Tatyana Tolstoya told you she thought the problem in Russia is from back before even the communism—most people in Russia were not even Christian: they believed in the spirits, in a force for instance in the corner of the room and there had been in Tolstoya's life—George was telling me what I had told him of going to see Tatyana Tolstoya in Maryland now many years ago and this man, Tolstoya was talking about, was talking about the spirit which lived in the corner of the room and how water had to be fed into the corner of the room. His language, I can not put it into English in a way that will make sense to you here sitting with me: but this man, this high and powerful figure in the KGB was talking about a spirit living in the corner of his office and he was not in any way embarrassed by this—

So, George was saying, that man I was telling you about, living in the apartment of a man he probably had a hand in murdering, was wearing the clothes of the murdered man and I had happened to have seen the murdered man at the opera and I remembered the red lined cape this man wore over his uniform and I saw that cape draped across the back of a chair in that room near the fireplace... it is the only way, you must know, that the man standing in front of me could know that this other man was really dead because *he* was now wearing the clothes of the dead man...

So, is there any way to understand these men—this man, please, because the plural denigrates while making it all too easy to forget such a man actually exists but how to really show what he thought and knew to be in the corner of the room, and on his back, George was saying, this man—call him Ivan, just like that agent of your story—was wearing the dress shirt, the jacket, the cloak of a man he had seen done to death, as sure as you are sitting across from me and I was supposed to believe that this man Ivan was in an apartment filled with furniture which had been in this man's family for a hundred years, while I knew very few families in Sofia went back a hundred years and certainly not Ivan who came from the country and it was ever present in his mouth when he talked to me in that clumsy way he had for someone who really did fear me for some reason—this man was a Minister and in the Central Committee and he had his hand really in the blood, as his best friend might whisper, George said, yet maybe he thought I could put the eye upon him—he had heard people call psychiatrists, soul suckers who could chop open a hole in a person's head and suck the soul out of it.

You must remember Ivan was a Communist and he believed far more deeply in the soul than any priest but don't get me wrong. Ivan was a modern man. He was looked on as one of the more reasonable people around Zhivkov, someone people thought to be intelligent and not a cruel person but he was standing there in the clothes of a man he had murdered and nothing was to be thought unusual about any of this. He was a concerned father who had a son who was a drunk and only wanted to die. I do not know how Ivan got my name. He didn't have to explain how he got my name. No one in Bulgaria would even waste time asking such a question. He gave me a glass of scotch and watched me drink from it. He himself did not drink but I knew I was expected to drink the scotch. No food was brought into the room and placed on the table. I told you this was a man who had traveled: have I told you that? He had been to Rome, he had been to Paris. He didn't like those cities. He had no real interest in being outside of Bulgaria. There was no reason for him to be outside Bulgaria. I drank half the scotch and Ivan said, do you think you could help my son? Ivan was standing behind the chair and I watched his hand tapping the top of the back of the chair where he should be sitting. There would be none of that looking into my eyes and us sitting opposite each other across the low table. I could feel the angle of his eyes looking down at me and the angle told me what I was to say as if I had any choice really in the matter. It was not a matter of choice in the way you possibly understand the word: do I go to work today, do I stay home, does my child go to public school or private school, do we buy a new car this year or wait until next, do I help my neighbor who asks if I can watch over his apartment while he is away...

You have to allow me to distance you from where this conversation—though it was more like an interview—but maybe you have more of an inkling than most Americans who are fortunate to have never been in such a situation and I do not criticize them for not having this experience as that is much too easy and so predictable on the part of people who really want to deny such a world as in Sofia in that moment might really exist and went on for so many years as if it was a normal way of life with just some minor difficulties due to the historical situation while in the actual reality of living in Sofia to even imagine the possibility of another sort of life was really grounds for declaring by Ivan and his even more brutal associates that such a belief as being the ravings of a diseased mind which was the actual thought in Bulgaria and described the mechanism for labeling people in that time—a sliver of the true inkling you had makes it uncomfortable to listen to me but if your listener is Bulgarian or an American who wants to always think the worst of his country's experience quickly begins to deny that nothing like that could really be happening in Bulgaria and if it was... well, anyway, it is just as bad in the United States or in England, didn't you know?

Was I prepared for the death of this man's son, was I the one who would be held responsible for the death of Ivan's son?

I hesitated.

Ivan was impatient. He had not expected my hesitation. That never happened with the people who were surrounding him on the Central Committee. But do not think I am being melodramatic though there is an element of it, I admit in this delaying and how obvious he must have thought as I was being so transparent in answering the question with a question... Your son, Ivailo—that's his name?—drives his car very fast?

And our dear Bulgarian roads protect his life since his cars are not built for them. (Ivan laughed at his own little joke) while the sidewalks of our capital have been known to rear up and slap him across the face but not before he says things that of course he does not believe but which can be misunderstood though as you well know the words of a drunk are without meaning but are believed by those who hear them as being the true thought of a man's...

Ivan caught himself and would not be lead into using the word *soul* or the word *heart* which I am sure he almost uttered as a substitute caught in his throat... and I watched his hand squeeze the top of the chair as if it was the neck of a chicken—the farmyard suddenly gripping me though surely the mud was long gone from my own shoes—: a very large hand that had not hesitated to remove from the closet the clothes he was wearing and which not many years before had been worn by the man who had been murdered. The clothes were worn with care and the inevitable little stains were quickly removed as somehow marking the passage of time. It takes a while for clothes to reshape themselves about the body of their new owner. I was always glad to be the oldest and so my clothes were passed to my brother though that is another story as I have also been thinking about him… The chair blocked my view of Ivan's shoes so I do not know for sure if he was also standing in that man's shoes in contradiction of that fake requirement for understanding how another person feels or thinks.

Ivailo is a danger to himself and to other people, I said aware of the banality of my sentence.

I do not care if he is a threat to other people. They can or can not take care of themselves. It is none of my concern.

I can talk to Ivailo if you wish but he must be sober if I am to talk with him.

A certain let down I am sure for you, for anyone who might hear my story and Ivan was relieved, I think. He did not have to think about Ivailo anymore, right now and right now is all that mattered in a mind such as Ivan's while he simply told me, You will be called.

Obviously I was not murdered, my family was not hurt, I did not lose my position at the academy: in fact nothing happened. Maybe Ivan simply forgot about me. He had summoned me. We had talked. He had shown his concern

for his son. He had tried to do his best for his son. He had
been really concerned about his son.

I never saw Ivailo. We all heard that this boy was on
the Riviera. The son of Zhivkov was on the Riviera. It was
a good destination for Bulgarian communists, better than
Switzerland. No one will believe you as you write about
Bulgarian communist children living on the Riviera. It
sounds too fantastic.

—so an obvious pause?—

—a pause to remember on page 45 the talking about
the German language… traveling, of course, is all about
languages though this is being written in American with the
possibility of being moved into other languages—maybe—
but there has to be a start or a turn as when I turned into
North G Avenue in Douglas, on another occasion: that
wide wide street heading south I guess I was aware of the
always going back, even George…

⋯→↑

And ever, against eating cares
   "L'Allegro" John Milton

The fickle pensioners of Morpheus' train
   "Il Penseroso" John Milton

George went back to Germany, after he was living in
New York, on two occasions as he would later say, but in

fact there was only one occasion he would bother to talk about. The two or it could have been three visits to Germany merged into one visit and that was enough for him.

Why go into what happened, he would say in the Grass Roots. I went back to Germany. I saw Otto. Was it in September, August or in March? Does it really matter? I saw Otto. Otto saw me.

This was back before George began to get sick, before things were going wrong with parts of his body. A series of illnesses, then parts of the body began to give out: they were repaired and then the repairs caused problems which necessitated stays of varying lengths in hospitals and though I never saw his back I do know it was covered by some sort of skin condition which never fully went away and for which there was no cure.

The language of the previous paragraph is stilted on purpose to allow for understanding how George described and then talked about the physical condition of his body. As a doctor he naturally looked at his own body as just another specimen on the examination table which always had the sure potential for becoming the autopsy slab.

⇢↑

From the days when George went to what was then called the DDR or the German Democratic Republic he had become friendly with a man named Otto. George was coming from the People's Republic of Bulgaria. Back then there were many visits by car, by train, even by plane. Of course it is always hard to look back at that time when, as you Americans say, pinpointing, sticking the wall to pin all the moments knowing someone and deciding this is the meeting in which someone passed over to the condition to be called friendship.

The word has a contaminated meaning in Bulgarian. When you see the word DRUSHBA, always there are those hands reaching from a space beyond the poster, up on the wall whether it is the wall of the Communist Party headquarters or the reduced wall behind the speaker's head in a local club meeting room where the comrades are just anxious to get back to the rakia after the presentation of the friendship, always undying, between the Bulgarian and Soviet people, between the Bulgarian and Soviet Party.

George heard on his visit to Germany—that is long after the fall of The Wall, an old record by DAF. Otto of all people quoted a line from one of the guys who sang in that group: *I don't believe in anything so I'm free to play with anything I want. We take all that we want and play with it.*

Of course it is the sort of nonsense Otto would quote and think I would be interested. He would quote from a song "Der Mussolini."

Und tanz den Mussolini

tanz den Adolf Hitler

beweg deinen hintern

und tanz den Jesus Christus

So far had Germany moved, George said. DAF: Deutsch Amerikanische Freundschaft.

But this time no corpse hands suspended in the air but

sweaty naked backs bending to a music that wanted a penis to go somewhere...friendship American style, German style...

Otto listens to no one but himself, you must understand, and he is a bad listener, much given to repeating himself and after the second beer all he does is repeat that he wants to be my friend and is afraid I will no longer be his friend and you remember when he came to New York all he wanted to do was sit in my kitchen and talk about our friendship and those years in what had been the DDR, when I would come to visit and we would go out to drink and look at the girls. I traveled with these friendship groups and we would be taken to hospitals to observe how our German... I can not use the word for what they called these doctors or clinicians... were treating the mentally ill. They had very good drugs in Germany. The Germans were always good with drugs. They invented heroin which is a very good drug... that is what is so strange about Americans... if people knew what a good drug heroin is... but that is not my problem. They didn't give their patients heroin. Their patients made a very neat bed. They piled their possessions on little tables next to their beds. All of them did this.

Otto worked in the laundry of a hospital in Berlin, of course then it was Berlin, the Hauptstadt of the DDR. Later after the Wall came down he moved to Hamburg.

During the Communism it was not unusual for a man like Otto to be working in a laundry. In Bulgaria smart people worked in many strange places. You went where they sent you. Otto maybe was not as smart as I thought originally. But he talked with me. He even came to Bulgaria from his work to the Black Sea. You can't imagine where they sent the people from the socialist countries. Ordinary people, you would say in the United States, would be sent as a group to a fraternal Socialist country for their holiday. They did not go to the best resorts on the Black Sea. Those were for the people from the capitalist countries who were spending real money.

Otto had been something other than a worker in the laundry, George said. Even after all the years, the meetings in Bulgaria, the meeting here in New York, I still did not know what he did before he worked in the laundry. Germans are like that. He had been married and was maybe still married but I never met his wife if he was still married, as he said she was away but she was always away when I saw him in Germany. I listened to Otto tell me how lonely he was, how afraid he was of getting older and older and then to be dying alone. He shouldn't have drank so much but I could only tell him this when he was drinking so there was no real point to it.

And you can ask why I was friends with Otto, to use the word he used when he called late at night… it was always late at night in his city… to hear his voice, that voice in the clarity of my coming back from listening to patients all day and it was always it seemed on the day when I saw patients all day, all day and having just sat down to listen to Ligeti while Vera was out alone as she wanted to be with her friends to whom I never had anything to say—and the phone rings: it is Otto telling me he thinks he has had a heart attack and he is dying and do you think this is natural that I can still talk, can still dial a telephone number and why am I so alone here, now and why are you so far away, George...

Otto would slur my name as if it was an uncommon name. It made me even more removed from him because it sounded pretentious when he said I was his only friend in the whole world which might have been true and that is what is so sad about Otto: he exaggerated the hard sound of the second G in my name—how preferable the name George is in English where the second G is softened—but at least he did not use the diminutive of my name: that would have been the straw cracking the camel's back—and Otto would ask me, as he always did, it seemed, but I might have been forgetting the times when he did not ask me but it seemed like he always asked me: George, do you believe in God? and he would say before I could answer him, I believe in God, but that night I shouted at him as he was speaking and I could hear him crying as I was shouting—which was very strange (a sort of whimpering sound)—or maybe I am imagining it, though I don't think so—I do not believe in God, that is it, I do not believe in God and Otto would be crying making these sounds with his voice like some awful screeching Arabic record, is all I could think of, and why did I say, Otto would be saying, such hurtful things and I would tell Otto that when you are dead you are dead and there are no other words for it—there is no God waiting to meet you.

The phone would fall out of his hand. I could hear him

reaching for it and the chair scraping on the wooden floor of his kitchen but suddenly in the manner of the seriously disturbed and with the most pleasant of voices he would ask me if the children were healthy, just like that, as if he had not asked me about God or anything else.

I remember doing nothing with Otto in Germany when I was visiting him. I knew not to stay with him as he wanted to have me as a hostage.

George would resist saying what he made of going to Germany. Having been to Germany, he would ask, you know what I mean. They are so easy to make observations about. You can always take pictures of them. They always provide those pictures. It is their nature, you could say. I have a photograph of Berlin from the air. It is on the cover of the Robbe-Grillet novel you gave me to read after I finished reading *Doctor Faustus*. Remember I read that before I went to Germany the first time after I was living in America and then I read a novel by Max Frisch—*Man in the Holocene*—I read it in German along with the English version Vera had read but that Max Frisch novel was not really preparation for going back to Germany except in that the experience of the novel in English and the experience of the novel in German are very different and maybe I should not have read both versions which is not the case with the other novel of Frisch's that I read: *Stiller*—I read that only in German because it seemed to be written inside the German language, one of my patients told me this as if I would know what he meant by that and in some way I think I understand what he meant since some books are only for those people within the language and you remember what it is like to be only inside a language—*Man in the Holocene*—I should not have read: I could wait a little while longer before I— do you know—no, you can not, know what it feels like to know you are carrying a piece of a pig inside your body and this piece of a pig is keeping you alive.

Of course Frisch is not German but I wanted to read something after *Doctor Faustus* so I could go to Germany because it seemed to say Germany was such a special place even though Mann I think wrote the novel in Los Angeles of all places and Los Angeles was a place that was impossible to go to again just as Germany was a place that Mann in his mind could not go to, the Germany that had created his mind—which is something Freud would have allowed but which his disciples would never suggest because you know disciples are always more rigid than their mentors. And then you forget you had this thought and go to Germany after reading the Max Frisch novel which is uncomfortable in another way.

The picture on the cover of the Robbe-Grillet novel *In the Labyrinth* is of a German city, where everything has been bombed down to rubble. A few buildings are still standing in a landscape mostly flattened when seen from the air.

Of course that is not the case in Germany today. When I would go to Berlin in those old days, from Bulgaria, you could still see all the open spaces… where something had been. In the West those spaces were filled in but in the East they had not been filled in. Now everything is mostly filled in. That is why maybe I like the modern music from Germany—

Heiner Goebbels, what a name! or Stockhausen—what is not there! A music of what is not there. When you would go to a concert in Sofia the music was always filled in, it was the usual classical music: everything filled in.

Can you tell me what we heard when we went to the Brooklyn Academy and heard and saw the piece by Heiner Goebbels? I am not asking you a quiz—but I can not remember anything beyond going with you and then Vera drove you back to Manhattan because it was very late… she was very angry with me because I would not wait until we got home to smoke a cigarette. No, I couldn't wait and the argument went its usual course, as I have told you…

I didn't tell you: Otto would take me to one place in Hamburg. He had a little garden on the outskirts, like many Germans have. Don't ask me how he got the little plot of land. He was telling me I would like his little farm because I was Bulgarian and someone had told him Bulgarians were good gardeners—they had the gift in their fingers, didn't Lydia tell you but you knew the way to make a Bulgarian angry is to accuse a city dweller of being a peasant which of course is true for most Bulgarians: they are peasants or just one generation from the land—and they do not want to be reminded of that, naturally.

Otto was proud of his garden but nothing much grew in his garden. He said something had happened to his plants and he was waiting for some sort of compensation from the man who had the plot of land next to his—over there and there had been an argument and letters were exchanged. The plot of land—is allotment the word in English?—had chairs and a little table and Otto brought beer and even bought for my visit a bottle of scotch for me to drink and I said I didn't like to drink scotch in the afternoon. And it was Johnny Walker scotch and I do not drink Johnny Walker scotch because that is the only scotch they drink in Bulgaria if they have access to the dollar shops, back then.

Otto knew so much and nothing. He was a man sinking into the earth. If you have a garden the plants maybe keep you up above the ground for a little while longer—even the legs of the chairs had sunk into the dirt… I was afraid he was going to talk about a Karl May novel. My mother had a German friend in Bulgaria who sent me a Karl May novel but I do not understand the German who likes such books. I was reading about Otto in the Max Frisch novel—or at least thought about him in a way, as if I…

You should know Otto is German. I came to America because I knew even if I had a German passport, and my children had German passports there was no way for us to become German, no matter how hard they try to make it easier now to become German. It is not like being here in America. Do not get me wrong: I do not dislike Otto. He was someone I knew, that is all.

→↑

After that going back to Germany, George didn't go back to Europe and should have gone into America he suggested or rather as he would say, the United States of America, but he did not beyond going out to the Hamptons because his wife had been invited out to stay there, but that was not an America he was able to understand, he thought, he told me, people in Bulgaria go to the Black Sea but does that place or that going reveal anything we can talk about, that is worth talking about… maybe I am limited in this, but I do not like to leave New York City, now, and I am stuck in Forest Hills which is not New York City—but one day, possibly— my office is in New York City there on Sullivan Street, that is New York City—Manhattan is New York City—and my wife cannot understand me for saying this.

> Mallarme who considered that the advent of photography revealed our destiny as "empty forms of matter'… made it resonate in his poems as if, to quote Yves Bonnefoy, he wanted to return via the photographic 'effect' to the mute appearance of things, performing an experiment in which the meaningless, hopeless absolute would then be absorbed in his self-consciousness now penetrated by its own Void.
>
> from *A Desire for Disposession: Portrait of the Artist as A Reader of Mallarme* by Remi Labrusse in PIERRE BONARD

THIRTYSEVEN

George.

↕ ←—

You might say it was inevitable that I, Karri, would remind you of what had brought us together: George
HE HELPED ME
Later we knew each other in peculiar ways in the so-called private world outside of his office. You never knew this and I think it was also the case of two other people who through him who did things in the arts.

Like Freud, George worshipped at the shrine of art... he once said. Though it is hard for anyone to connect the word *worship* with George, a man more brutal than your namesake, Thomas, in his absolute belief in the actual matter that can be touched, weighed, tasted: the essential apparent contradiction to his mind work.

↕ ←—

He was spun... what a curious phrase... People say I heard a kid saying this on the pier in Santa Monica. The kid seemed to know what he was speaking of: spun, I would think like cotton candy, granules of sugar spit out and blown into fluff about a cardboard baton at a street fair stand. More likely, a way to describe a kid falling down or going who knows where.

George was like that.

You figure it out yet?

Of course George will not be in Los Angeles. He is dead.

Really dead, as one has to say.

But can I be sure? (Just for the sake of argument.)

George would have no doubts about any of this.

When you are dead you are dead.

For the weeks when he was in the hospital at the end they gave him the drug that stops your brain from thinking, from remembering, from dreaming.

So I would be dead before I was dead, he had been saying…

No mouth can utter those words.

They stick a pig valve in me and give me rat poison to keep the blood flowing.

What a world, right, George was saying. I tap my chest and imagine the foreign thing in me, that thing is keeping me alive as long as I take the rat poison and then it didn't work or something else happens as it always does and as George knew from his medical studies: the sure slide into the morgue.

⇕⇕

Ahead and behind what I am trying to tell you.

You don't have to believe a guy like me, Karri, could have run into George and then run into you and George had stayed in touch with me, and with whom I visited back in New York, someone other than my friend who lived near you… once in Hermosa Beach as that is where I am from, as if you could have figured it out but probably you didn't.

↕

Don't for a moment think you will *get* Los Angeles. You need one of those bound up Thomas street guides and set yourself to reading it day after day while you are waiting for your Dad to conduct business with the men he is hiring to fix up the house he is buying at the end of a road that takes a long time to get to. You need to figure out how one road leads to another. You can't read a map and drive. It doesn't work that way even today and I don't care if you have one of those remote guidance systems. When you use them you don't see anything, you spend all your time listening and being told what to do.

↕↯

Let me tell you, the night when George and I walked down to the ocean past all the new houses—he wouldn't know they were new houses or old, it was the first time I had taken him down there, but he knew what I was talking about as I was telling him they are wiping out what I had walked midst as a kid. I don't know any of these people. I guess they're okay but you don't see them during the week for the most part and they don't say hello and it's a different place, now, like everyplace I guess. They put up these big places and don't really live in them; just one of their houses and they probably can't keep track of them or even have to but I still walk down to the ocean even though I know it is always here, nothing to be done with it which is a consolation in a way for something or other.

But something came from George which I take to calling *The Shroud*.

↕ ↵

Recollection at times fills up the room, he was telling me, even here sitting on the wall at the edge of the beach with our backs to that big obscene house which always had half-naked kids lounging around the big gas fed fireplace— didn't the guy, who owned the house, wasn't he some sort ofHollywood big shot?—looking at the ocean *out there* though George said he would rather be looking at the big house which that night did not have the lounging kids and was rather desolate, to tell the truth, a certain sentimental sadness to a folded up sunshade hanging down from a pole like a drooping penis: I had been asking, George said, in Bulgaria—that year when he was there for the whole year—about what had gone on in the concentration camps under the Communists. I can't keep track of the pronouns, so forgive me. He was interested in the camp of Lovech because it was near Pleven where he grew up. He had been surprised the executioners and the victims both wanted to forget their times in the camp. He had been told of an incident which happened with certain regularity. There would be the usual roll-call in the morning after which the men were issued with shovels and other tools but on certain days one man would be issued, in addition to his shovel or rake, a large dirty piece of canvas, that he was expected to carry all day as he went about his assigned digging in the field. This was nothing new. He and everyone knew what was coming.

Suddenly, sometime during the day, the man carrying the piece of canvas would be set upon by the guards and slowly and methodically beaten to death with long clubs. The other prisoners and guards would watch this activity. The body would later be rolled onto the canvas and taken away. No one remembered any sound ever being uttered by the guards, the other prisoners or now, the dead man.

This activity never varied except for one time which was mentioned by three people George talked to.

One day the commandant who always participated in the beatings brought along his son who must have been around 11 or 12 years old. The boy was forced to stand close to his father and while he was not allowed to beat the prisoner he was still splashed with the victim's blood and it seemed so calculated, these people said, because they remember very specifically how the father had drawn a line in the dirt and told his son to stand behind it, not to move, no matter what.

This detail of calculation was what held George and how, while people mentioned it, there was never a second of refection upon what it might mean. There was a polishing of the detail as if that is all that mattered. It could have been that people or the people I talked to did not have sentences to describe what they had seen beyond the facts of what they had seen.

George was sure I could imagine the man carrying the piece of canvas or possibly the boy standing behind the line in the earth, but you were not there so it might allow your imagination to… though that is unfair… allow your imagination to give more meaning to this man, this son and the man—one of many—who was being beaten to death.

We want to give meaning to their actions. We want them to be thinking. We want them to have feelings about what is happening—and here I have really entered into that man's head: this is happening and he is aware of it happening but he is not holding the club. The club is being held and it is being swung over the head. There are sounds. There is a man being beaten. There will be a dead man. The body will be wrapped up. It will be carried away.

Can I show you anymore clearly what has happened? The boy will have found blood on his jacket sleeve, maybe on the front of the jacket, maybe on his trousers. He will change his clothes and he will wear clean clothes. He is expected to wear clean clothes. This is something he knows and it is a bother to change his clothes but he will change his clothes because his mother provided him with clean clothing.

Nothing is out of the ordinary. That is what I discovered talking to men who witnessed these actions, who participated in these actions. They did not even use the word actions. Think about it as if you tried to remember even one person you saw specifically this morning when you went to buy the newspaper at the 7/11. I am not thinking if you ran into someone you knew but try to remember some person you saw this morning... maybe waiting for the bus...

Of course I know and you know now something happened in the camp, something that is shocking, disturbing and wrong but to the people I talked to in Sofia it was like my going to the subway or your walking down to the ocean...

↕↳

I know or knew where Bulgaria is, Karri is saying, because I was living in Turkey for two years though I knew where Bulgaria was even before that though I knew well enough turkey was something that came with cranberry sauce if I went along the street asking people if they knew where Turkey was, you mean where is the turkey?

←↕

George liked Los Angeles and insisted Vera and he leave it as soon as possible. They had intended staying there for a month or so, Karri was saying. Bulgarians had pushed their way West over the years and some were now rich, rich, rich enough to be famous all the way back in Sofia.

It had always been unclear how this man had made the money qualifying him to be described as being rich in California, but it was always said in the same way: Vetgo had become rich in California.

No one bothered to ask where in California and how this transformation had happened.

Occasionally an address had been passed around very quietly as in the outdoor café out behind the television station, you know out beyond the restaurant *Under the Lime Tree*... Remember, George was saying to Vera, when you discovered a nephew of your mother's—who was it—and he gave us a good table and even made sure the meat was fresh and not that indescribable stuff they saved for people they did not know and who they eventually had to serve if only because there were limits, even in a restaurant, for how long you could make someone wait.

Maybe, it was in California where George discovered that it was nearly unbearable to use the verb, *remember*, because he was aware in California and in particular in Los Angeles: all you were supposed to do was think about other places, other times.

Why was this so? A fitting question for a question and a question of a question that might been cracked with two consecutive days of rain, an experience George never had in Los Angeles.

If people could train themselves not to compare where they were at the exact moment with what was in their pasts, train themselves to avoid running the peripheral slide show as they drove those beautiful freeways—Los Angeles would appear as the wonderful place where he knew he might have even been happy, but now it was too late: the verb *remember* banging on his head and Vera really had to find that Bulgarian, she had heard about in Sofia, related in some way to her father's uncle and remember we had met his nephew up on Vitosha: the wife worked in some ministry she didn't talk about and you didn't ask or make insinuations that such work was only possible because this wife had something on someone who…

One freeway after another freeway lead to a house up in one of the sets of hills, the name of which George no longer could keep track of, a house set off by itself and surrounded with a large piece of land which had been covered with tiny coloured pebbles arranged carefully in parallel columns with no obvious significance though he was not going to be inclined to ask, if it came to that: what was the thought behind the colours and the care taken in arranging the pebbles? He would not encourage this man in the common belief that everything we do has a meaning, has a significance that can be explained but in a language quickly becoming very soft, gooey almost as when, for instance that girlfriend of Vera talked about the "meaning" and you were supposed to put quotation marks, I am sure, George would say, around both the word meaning and then the words that glibly came and could just as easily be describing the colours of bath-tubs on display at Home Depot as they were now being used to describe these bracelets this woman wore to show aspects of the meanings in her individual life.

The field of pebbles was surrounded by a high iron fence painted a dull green as if it was to contain a cell behind it. George noticed barbed wire strung in curlicues along the top of it. You usually did not see barbed wire in New York City except in a display about the making of the American

West that he went to at the Museum of Natural History with his children, when he did such things and they were not allowed to have more important things to do. There had been a small case in which maybe thirty or so different types of barbed wire were arranged in three columns. I cannot tell you the poetic sounding names for each of those strands and how the variety in such a simple thing captured the interest.

His patients—even those who had no firsthand experience of the camps—often talked about barbed wire and how it was part of their dreams he was expected eventually to explain though he avoided the ploy of asking his patients what they thought the barbed wire meant…

Vera did not have a telephone number for this man and she had been told all you had to do was show up. The rich people in California were very different, she had been told, but there were no details to go along with this distinction.

Near the gate was a sign pointing to a button with directions:

PRESS BELL ONCE.
STEP BACK
YOU ARE BEING PHOTOGRAPHED.

George did not argue with Vera but went back to the car. She rang the bell and the door opened. In the car with the windows open on all sides, he smoked.

And waited.

And waited.

There were other houses surrounded by various barriers up and down the sloping street. Palm trees reared up and up in such a way that one look and not again, he thought, as in New York, one look up at the skyscrapers to get it out of the system.

Rich people in California, behind their iron fence speaking Bulgarian about how much they enjoyed their lives now that they were in California. One felt almost new, they were saying, the two of them, while Vera eager and wanting to join in and knowing it was a good thing George didn't come inside. She saw the expression on his face from all her talk of their feeling like new… just so much…and remembering where they had come from and what they had gone through, remember, remember though, Vera demanded: what if it was true?

The rich people who will not acquire a name—other than Vetgo—as George could not be bothered to learn their actual names—it was sufficient, they could be known as the rich people in California, who felt: they were almost new people but only once to Vera he would ask: don't they have mirrors midst all their possessions? Who are they kidding and always the first person deceived is yourself.

She would smirk, if you had come inside the house maybe…

I like sitting in the car, George would say and leave off his story telling or his telling and my listening always wrapped around:

And he helped me.

Let me tell you: you remember the time in Rosa's, that time at the table toward the back of the room to the left of where they kept the cash register.

I don't like sitting close to where they keep the money. You never know when someone is going to come in to make a withdrawal. George would think I was crazy or something and he would look to you to agree since you were both from New York.

George didn't finally mind, Karri said, the geographic provincialism of Americans. He was not prepared to go down the usual path: do you think most of my neighbors on Driggs Avenue could name any state in the United States beyond say New Jersey and even that place was a pretty strange idea to them... they fly in from Pakistan, from Poland, from Bulgaria even and I often wonder how they find themselves there and how they got from the airport and then they turn around and once or twice a year go back the way they came. They look neither to the right nor to the left. They do not think to go beyond where they have ended up and when they are back *in my country* as they call it they talk about their lives in New York because no one in those places knows anything about Driggs Avenue in Brooklyn or that strange name Brooklyn which is more just the name of a type of cheap Italian chewing gum... remember, don't you,

Medy talking that night of getting stuck with BROOKLYN chewing gum because she couldn't read the name on the package though she knew it was not in Bulgarian so it had to be good gum since it was not Bulgarian gum—what they tried to pass off as chewing gum right down to putting the name FLORIDA on the package but she knew that trick and her customers knew that trick after one bite into the Bulgarian stuff… Medy would not use the appropriate curse word for it and just a click of the tongue and a spit that did not produce any spray told a person what she thought of the FLORIDA gum.

This was before the falling out with George, when Medy was looking after his children in the afternoon: it was only a brief moment, but George was aware that when Medy was in the apartment it was as if the whole country of Bulgaria had arrived and crammed itself into every cranny of the apartment. Breathing became hard and George had his tongue tied into the knot his patients often talked about just before the instant when the words came pouring out but as he looked about the apartment all he could think about were the frontiers of the People's Republic of Bulgaria and while he knew eventually that the name of the country changed it was also back when he knew Medy and while, she was not in any real sense part of the People's Republic of Bulgaria, her presence reminded him of the breath holding all Bulgarians went through as they passed by train, car, bus or plane out of the country, across the frontier, across the border into outside.

It didn't matter if one crossed the frontier into Yugoslavia or into Romania though these were the only frontiers he himself had passed through by land… he could feel the land scraped clean along the dust darkened corners of the rooms on Driggs Avenue while remembering pictures from the films they had been required to watch which depicted the heroic work of the frontier guards who were ever vigilant in protecting the borders of the People's Republic of Bulgaria.

The breath holding was a little more strenuous when passing into Yugoslavia for all such obvious reasons, as you well know, but even to go into Romania—which was a country that was a little unreliable—produced the breath holding and George knew he was not unique in this and while he nodded his head when Medy talked—did she ever stop talking?—always nonsense, for sure, about things that had not happened or things that had happened on Botev Boulevard in the famous kiosk in Sofia.

←···←···

George had seen the one photo that existed of Medy when she had just come from the countryside to Sofia as the war was coming to an end and she had a flat cart with piles of something on it—some sort of nut—sunflower seeds, possibly and it was parked near the train station. He did not know where she lived or how she had gotten to Sofia from the countryside but it was a fact that she had lived longer in the capital than he had lived there but the manner of her sitting at the table in the kitchen there on Driggs Avenue, with her back erect, not supported by the back of the chair, sitting on the corner of the chair with her legs spread and even in summer wearing heavy stockings, sweat pouring from her brow…

◄┄┄┄►

George was sure Medy did not believe she was in New York. Of course she knew her body was here in Brooklyn but everything else was still in Bulgaria: she was in Bulgaria, she Medy. She could say a few words in English but she could have said those few words of English in Sofia, and a few words in German, in French—but they meant nothing except the smile on the face of the person who was listening to her.

In no way, George is saying, am I having some sort of mystical experience or talking about time travel or having a sense a person can be in two places at once.

Many people travel the world but everything about their way of understanding the world does not allow them to acknowledge they have ever really left what is, or gone beyond in Medy's case, the frontiers of Bulgaria or the place they came from.

I cannot be in the same room with her. All these years have been in vain. The years in Germany, the years here in Brooklyn, the traveling about in the United States of America… for all of that—seeing Medy, hearing her voice I find myself in Pleven where my grandmother never stopped talking about the rain. I do not mean she talked about the weather like many people… no, she talked about the rain and she talked about the rain; it was the only thing she could talk about anymore. It had rained, it was raining, it would be raining. The actual weather did not matter. There was only rain.

That woman is as dead as yesterday and becomes Medy sitting at the kitchen table.

Didn't you say once, George was saying, poetry should be as well written as prose and you said you were not playing with words because you despised people who played with words or talked about playing with words. Someone might think I was playing with words when I talked about my grandmother but I was only trying to show what Medy did to me.

←⋯↑

Do you remember how Medy treasured the little calendar she got from the Bulgarian Orthodox Church which listed the old saint's days and the important feast days of the church? I do not know how she managed to get it here in New York. She had a life her daughter, that you, and I knew nothing about. The clerical almanac would show up in early December. She did not go to the Bulgarian church in New York so how did she ever get a copy? She never went by subway anywhere though she seemed to know people who would appear as if conjured out of thin air, if I can say it without being mysterious in any way.

In no way was Medy mysterious to me. She was as plain… and just there as those women you would see in the Sofia train station with their baskets which had a piece of cloth sewn across the top. Two baskets, always in front of them and then they would be gone to be replaced by more of these women…was I supposed to imagine what went on in their minds?

No one had ever done so. Intellectuals in the old days would go to the countryside and try to enter into the mind of the peasants. They would bring back songs and music. There would be claims tracing the words and motifs back to Homer or some such far away… you know about the famous experiments in Yugoslavia?—in Bulgaria they had to work harder and the results? As interesting as the dead animal skins on the floor of Yavarov's museum house.

This was during the time when they carved out the brain from the corpse of Ivan Vasov and put it into a big jar, you remember? that place behind the National Theatre, taking a break from the Bambouk to look at the brain of a genius. They did the same thing to Lenin and Einstein.

Relics for non-believers.

Don't be too harsh on me for that misplaced pronoun, that paranoid pronoun. If I had a dollar for every time someone was talking about *them* or how *they* were planning or had already done something and how *they* never gave you a break or you had to know *them* before anything was likely to go your way.

At first, George was saying, I tried to keep track of the third person pronoun but very quickly and inevitably I lost track of who was being talked about. It would go on for weeks, for months. Each person talking about a they or them. Not that this was the only thing the patients would talk about but even for the rare patient that did not talk about these shadowy people at first I could always count on their eventual appearance in the fifty minutes, one of the weeks... every patient is different in how they come to trust you. Part of that trust arrives when they bestow their enemies upon you, share—how I hate that word—*them* with me and I always resist the natural response of refusing their offer.

That is what they pay me for: I am their storage space, their locker in the train station—fewer and fewer of those so that in a few years no one will know what I am talking about if I think of myself as a storage locker...I will have to become a storage space for these misplaced pronouns... but I hear their words carving grooves almost across their foreheads; the corners of a woman's eyes dissolve into a fan of at first faint lines but the years will dig them deep into those intimations...

So, I listen and every once in a while say something. The words are choked out of me:

and then

what did you feel

how did you experience

have you thought
might you be
are you sure
what if
but
however
and then
what did you feel
how did you
might you be
what if
however
have you thought
might you be

There are times when I strangle the smirking tone, any
hint I am repeating myself, as surely I am repeating myself.
Did you once tell me about a professor who fell asleep as he
was talking in his class: really fall asleep and not a black
out from drinking or drugs or any sort of brain damage: he
had just heard himself so many times say the same things
over and over again he found himself asleep with his eyes
wide open, his mouth working but aware he was asleep and
it was no metaphor for what he was doing as he well knew
what a metaphor was even if his students no longer knew
what it was, or had ever known, or even cared that they
didn't know what it meant… the mind drifts while a patient
is talking and when I was younger I worried about missing
something but I quickly realized if it was important it was

going to be repeated and repeated: there could be no doubt about it—and this is one of those things people do not understand—it is not my job to find the tiny detail that in the language of the television is going to explode a patient's mind into some sort of glow of understanding and only The Trained and Skilled Doctor is capable of digging that sentence out, or that phrase, or that fragment and only I, The Skilled Compassionate Professional, would be able to do this and then be able to hear it and if called upon...

Yet it does not matter what I am hearing. My ears are not the necessary receptacle for the patient's words.

How utterly wrong headed is that understanding—but a room filled with people probably does invite sleep and I am not surprised by the professor who you said took away no memories of his twenty-five years of teaching.

What is unusual about any of that... teaching is a form of work I discovered when I taught at the high school where the children went. I discovered while I did not under-estimate the interest the students would have in the course I did not expect my own hostility toward the experience and in no way were the students at fault... the provocation of their ignorance and their unawareness of their own stupidity were all things I knew from Bulgaria where under the communism stupidity was raised to new heights and made powerful when even the communists would consult with Vanga who people claimed could predict the future…a blind semi-literate peasant woman being courted by our rulers who are supposed to be rational scientific materialists… because they think she can predict the future. They sit there and listen to her nonsense: the world is going to end in 2079. Their heads nod and they walk away nodding.

Now, they know something.

No stupidity surprises me. This has been a century of murderous stupidity and it is no wonder psychoanalysis came along at the time it did. One form of nonsense to answer the many nonsenses proliferating in Vienna: a Petri dish of stupidity, foolishness, clever and not so clever nonsense.

You have seen the blood stained Archduke's tunic: remember you sent me a post card of it? All the wise rulers of Europe fall into the sewer that is Yugoslavia. I am sure there is a trashy play that puts Hitler in a railroad waiting room with Freud where they talk about Karl May, while Einstein wanders inappropriately in and laughs with his own memories of reading about Old Shatterhand.

But all those lives are complete. We have them to do what we want with them which is another sort of falling into a hole out which no one can climb. But the patient is to know none of this…even if it is nothing.

As George talks I am aware that there is no place for his voice. He is dead and without a place: not even a grave to tend to, to bring our memories. Probably just a box in the closet because it was even for his wife too heartless to reply to the undertaker: you can keep the ashes. George was not interested in ashes or in dead bodies or in those sorts of things.

When you are dead you are dead. The living carry enough around with them as it is: just to be alive...

How I hope, George says, that I will fade immediately from the memories of my children. I want to be erased from their lives, a hope as impossible as the future longed for by the statues all over Bulgaria that got toppled over with the change...

lurch

George is dead. Dead. Dead. Dead. Dead. Dead. Dead. Dead. Dead. Dead. Dead. Really dead. Dead. Dead. Dead. Dead. Dead. Dead. Dead. Really dead.

Dead, dead, dead, dead, dead, dead, dead, dead, dead, dead, dead, dead, dead

You told me, I called up the institute on 11th Street where George had worked. The receptionist said she was new and didn't know George but if I wanted I could talk to her supervisor who has been here a long time.

After more phone calls I was talking with the supervisor who at first didn't know who I was talking about or she was just being careful since after all this was a psychoanalytic institute and I could have been anybody: who knows and here was this guy talking about a dead therapist and something about a memorial service, as if she knew what he was getting at and did he want to have a memorial service or was he looking for... and I was saying I knew George had worked at the institute for many years and had known him for many years before that and was just wondering if there had been a notice in the newsletter, which I knew from the most recent one there had not been one and she was saying she remembered George but he had passed away and there hadn't been any memorial notices for him and she didn't know if one was planned but she doubted there would be, he died a long time ago, now, last year or something like that... he had been here for a long time but she didn't really know him that well and everything you have told me is new so I guess I am not the best person to talk to and I can't think of anyone I can refer you to but if I hear of anything I will call you and of course she hasn't called so I am again saying: George is dead. Dead. Dead. Dead. Dead.

Really dead and he is gone or is he gone in the sentimental sense of that phrase, George is gone but not...

yet there is no grave, no death notices peeling from lamp posts or walls and George is dead.

You say so what?

And I said, George is dead.

As dead as any person who is dead.

But shouldn't you get over the simple fact: George is dead. He wouldn't have given a thought to those death notices that went up on fences, walls, lamp posts in Bulgaria at set moments after a person died and I don't know the schedule of mourning though I do know there are different notices for the announcement, for the first month, the six months, the year and how you are supposed to go to the cemetery and have a meal on the grave or pour vodka or rakia or mastika, whatever it is the guy liked to drink and maybe you could even stuff a cigarette into the soil and here were those boxes you sometimes saw at the foot of the grave where the feet of the person would be down six feet: more like little cupboards on stilts where hoarded food is placed for the dead guy and of course it would eventually rot and have to get cleaned out by that relative who liked to keep the gravesites clean because you never know and then the years pass... the relatives are all dead. The boxes begin to rust and...

No, George is dead and there were no ashes. He was cremated through one of those services on Bleecker Street. He wasn't religious and Vera could see herself looking into his dead face in a coffin and what was the point: George didn't believe in any of that and there was a sort of memorial at his office at 104 Sullivan Street, between Prince and Spring on the west side of the street... pictures on the wall of him when... Friends, relatives, acquaintances don't all just die when someone dies. The common question: why him and not them...

You learn, George would say but not really, as you well know, there are questions that exist only as questions and they are the sort of questions rising up and banging you on the head like the most awful hangover...back to that again...

Here is a lurch to a place: George never had hangovers.

People live, people die. It would be awful if everyone lived forever...

⇥↔

I have been your unreliable narrator. I can't even keep track of the chapter breaks. Well, it is L.A., something like New Jersey...when I drive over to Torrance I know when I am there and have left Hermosa Beach, but if you asked me exactly when: do the same thing in New Jersey some day. It is not like in Chicago where they still got those nigger patrols. Who is saying this?

⇥↕

There are always loose ends: George once said he signed a paper in Sofia and someone was put in a hospital. It was not a bad hospital and he was probably safer there, though I did not ask after him because that would hurt, him you understand, *they* noticed if someone asked after someone they were interested in. Also, George would say for people what they wanted him to say when he testified downtown in New York at deportation hearings. They paid him to say

96

some things. He did not make up things. He said what they had told him. They wanted to stay in the United States. I would not have to see them. But the boy who was put in the hospital would have died in the army...

⋯➤⬅⋯

I suppose that is enough for the moment. George will always be of interest... how glibly, always, you won't find the Fabulous Zuckerman Sisters on the computer. I had hoped, but they did not appeal to homosexuals who are the guardians of much of our memories, if memory serves me right.

⋯➤⋯➤

His friend Thomas has another version of George. When Thomas came to Los Angeles, he wanted me to go to the desert with him. I refused. He asked me why I didn't go to the desert as he liked going to the desert. I put him off forever his telling me what he found in the desert.

These people from the East. It is either the ocean or the desert. I told Thomas when I have gone to the desert I have come back from the desert.

There is no difference between going and coming. That stopped the conversation or the drift of the conversation.

beginning

Inevitable.

Inevitability.

I cling to my casket as a way of knowing I am alive.

Three men sitting at the end of the bar in The Grass Roots on St Marks Place New York.

George worked with blood because he did not have the money to buy the medical exam from the Russian Jews in Brighton Beach.

Why did you keep all this stuff in your tiny room?

George would fight with his wife.

The words grew like ulcers in his head. Gerhard Roth.

Using the word very as in I feel very alone introduces a note of either comedy or bathos.

There was a mystery at the center of George's life.

Thomas, Ed and Joe sat at the end of the bar.

It seems he never mentioned Tanya, had he? A woman he was for long years with. She was older. She had not divorced which was hard for him. She was a colleague. I wonder how she is. She was very energetic and very non-standard, can I say that?

Let us go to Arizona to die.

The sure mathematical probability of having to make the arrangements as the chairbound Mr. Beckett replied to a question by Montague: and the arrangements?

In the ground.

Young people do not move to Arizona.

So, away from uncomprehending young people who have not listened to a death rattle as once you have heard a death rattle, you are never young again, you are always aware of the stupid look on your own face as you listened and then there was nothing, really nothing—and that is what the rattle is—the settling of the organs—physiologically speaking—followed by the nothing—the adolescent snickering so vacant you can only conclude there just has to be something meant by it though of course there is nothing—it is the laughter of the young who remain young… a certain muddle and hoping the mind will sufficiently dim before the arrival of the Spanish speaking hands, nearly a sure thing: only a very few are paying for English speaking hands.

The cemetery is the only permanent place in an American city.

During the communism the cemetery in Sofia maintained the only unpoliticized contemporary history of Bulgaria.

At one time, everyone had seen **ZORBA THE GREEK** and watched the old women tear apart the possessions of the recently dead.

George died at five A.M. in Columbia Presbyterian Hospital.

He had been in the ICU for more than five weeks.

His son and daughter were holding hands with their father.

His wife sat by the bed.

While George had signed a form saying no radical measures were to be taken, his wife asked the hospital to try to resuscitate him.

They closed the curtains having asked the children and the wife to step away.

I will never forget the sounds I heard, his wife said.

Stayed at this falling apart motel out near the Tombstone City Cemetery, the one they began to use when Boothill got filled up. In the early morning two stagecoaches would go by on the way to Allen Street where they transport visitors up and down the town: would have been interesting but they installed a third row of seats in the coaches. The scene has been seen often enough: the pretty girl, her elderly aunt, the salesman, the grumpy old guy, the young man who is up to either good or not: each then forced to look at the other but now lined up like sitting statues of Chinese funerary art… you had a choice to look at what you had passed or were going to pass…giving people what they want, the ticket seller said.

At my parents' graves, trying to imagine the stew of their corpses down there. The forensics of decomposition.

How many people remember having met my parents who have now been dead for more than 25 years?

Indulgent sentimentality.

George was saying, if I could erase myself from the memory of my children…

As I was driving across the Tohono O'odham reservation:

Quijotoa's post office was established December 11, 1883 and discontinued August 31, 1942. Discovered in 1883 by Alexander McKay, the mine responsible for Quijotoa was not all it was played up to be. Several thousand people flocked to the town but only a few years later it was deserted. There were over 20 saloons yet no jail. Lawbreakers were tied to a tree and shipped off the next morning to Tucson. A fire destroyed much of the town in 1889 and today, nothing remains.

George would fight with his wife. It was my smoking. My drinking. My music. My books. My art. My friends. My work.

My life is that what she was talking about?

My life, as if I have a life? What does she mean? Am I not supposed to have a life, my life?

Maybe what she means: your life, your precious life with its precious books, with its precious music: as if you will ever listen to all the music you have copied, as if you will ever read all the books you have ever bought? Do you think the children have read even one of the books you bought for them, all the way through? Can you tell me that? Is what she asks me?

Is it fair? I ask you. Is it fair for my wife to ask me such questions? All the books I have brought into the house— not one of them has she ever opened, even out of curiosity, a curiosity a cat might even have—but maybe I am being unfair? She does read but never has she read a book I have brought into the house.

And of course, the music? I can see on her face when she comes home and I am listening to what she calls *that* music of yours. How can you call it music, that music of yours? Raw sounds of helicopters, you said it was. How can you call that music or the screeching of machines?

Surely, you know better? Is that what she really did say? Surely, you know better?

The three men sitting at the end of the bar. A country court. The accused will be brought in. It has not been a busy day. Not a lot of coming and going.

The three men in a Poussin painting.

The three men in…

I wish it all were an awful dream and when I awaken… and again when I woke up from the false initial waking up because we all now find ourselves with many endings, many beginnings with whatever it is between lost somewhere within one of the endings or beginnings.

George under it for all those five weeks, medicated so as to prevent dreaming or memory but I can imagine my deathbed with the picture of Melinda, not there and George stopping me: more mawkish, can I say that, sentimental rubbish worse than a girl looking for a tall dark man from her novel with the quiet smile and kind eyes, an imagined death: the sheer triviality, how brave you are is the expected comment, to go where none had gone before

Only a grave can contain such thoughts. No living person would have the patience, even one in love: another valued aspect of the hole in the ground

Obituary writers imagine that they can summon up the whole course of a life. But they know nothing…Patrick Modiano. You have done these dreary calculations of visits, revisits once before in September 1984 when you counted on your fingers your last visit to Istanbul back in 1967 not realizing you would be there once again only a year later for a few weeks but now from 1985 to the moment of this…24 going on 25 years… no one else on this Sunday in January walking around the center of the world : LA MORTE D'UN POETE

Filling up the minutes, George, I could say, waiting for you to come meet me, or had you just left The Grass Roots—what night?—a Wednesday of course—remember, there came a time when you weren't sure anymore of feeling like it and things started to get in the way of your coming and it got harder and harder to persuade yourself of the long ride back—you never carried a book or newspaper, never, your hands were always empty—on the subway to Forest Hills: was it worth it sitting for an hour in a bar drinking three or four glasses of scotch—even Johnny Walker which sometimes the café/bar in Sofia—your ordering the Johnny Walker always recalled this café/bar for me—across from Sveta Nedelya had in stock on a glass shelf behind where the bartenders stood—and then the long ride, that long ride—though there were times when your friend with that peculiar name sounding like Venice:::: Vantzeti was coming to meet you, keep you company on the long ride out to Forest Hills and I always thought of a moment in Venice itself when I was first there with Lydia and we were walking near Campo San Stefano and hearing Bulgarian asking Lydia, Bulgarski? and she saying, Yes, but don't say anything to them you don't want to say anything to any Bulgarian you meet outside of Bulgaria until you find out why they are outside Bulgaria, but in the little café across from the black church that had been blown to bits by communist insurrectionists in 1925 and rebuilt stone by stone so as to disguise and remember—but I wanted to talk about this bar/café where the deaf and dumb students came from their training school to sign, I guess you would have to say, about what was going on as I remember it, but clearly this creeped out George (I wish there was a more eloquent way of describing his dismissive hand gesture and tone of voice)—who claimed once was enough having gone there by accident in all the years of his life in Sofia because they sold Johnny Walker that particular day, you are right about that, for some reason one bar or another would have a certain foreign liquor and there was never any rhyme or reason as might be said while I had gone there every night for one of the weeks I had been in Sofia during the winter, living in the front room of Medy's apartment on Vitosha Boulevard, when there was much snow on the ground and stepping into the café: so quiet except for the glasses being washed and the door opening and closing and yet full of people signing to each other… George could see no point in my going again and again to the café for the deaf and dumb and while I could not really articulate what had possessed me beyond the old clichéd inability of heaving the heart into the mouth, the inability to find words and while I knew signs were words they seemed clearer and possibly free… such nonsense, I didn't have time for, George would say: I never had a patient who was really struck dumb, never in all my years… but in that café/bar into which they came not able to have heard the snow being crunched by their boots or the trams scratching against the tracks as they curved about the church… I wanted them to be able to say, to sign better than I had been… George's head would now shake and his right hand would flick away what I had said: that café/bar is not there anymore, it has not been there for a long time… an accident of a winter's night in Sofia and you unlike all of the people in that café/bar, unlike too many people in Sofia you would be able to fly to Vienna later that month so as to spend New Year's in a refugee camp, not as a resident but as a sneaked-in guest of Medy's daughter and nephew, all just so fantastic and beyond the imagination of ninety-nine out of a hundred people you will meet even on the streets of New York City: to be dead is to be free of all these eccentric details that clutter the mind, that make the mind human, a mind that longs to be beaten by the single-minded whips because you know the hand, the single hand while here in the United States of America and now in Bulgaria, so long after that time... a nostalgia for the whip.

Obituary writers imagine that they can summon up the whole course of a life. But they know nothing...
Patrick Modiano.

Yeah, well... Karri says. He would, now wouldn't he? Does it matter in the slightest? Give yourself pause: you have become distracted toward the end, toward the coming to the end—and I reject any sexual allusion in that coming—we are here and too quickly I slid over my saying about George: he helped me.

Of course, he helped many people and it goes without saying, I am sure, though it probably matters no more than the reality of the wind clearing the cemeteries of the buckets of plastic flowers as they bulk up against the barbed wire enclosing the final resting places for...

George helped me.

He did not fix me.

He did not make me a better person.

George cleared away a lot of underbrush or got me, as the process suggests, to do this sort of basic work. He would have wanted you to finish up the stuff about Medy. And so much other stuff, always gathering more stuff, more

allusive every day, every moment you could say: how to
how to
with no slew of words to rest the
eye on—taking a rest, a pause—while the brain caught up
with the movement of the words... crap words, I have to
admit: *process, work to do on myself.*

you have to organize what you're saying so people won't
get confused, the best way is to keep telling the story in
terms of the dead, I said to him, it's very easy to talk but
bringing order to what you are saying isn't so easy (83/4)
Christ Versus Arizona by Camilo Jose Cela

None of this, none of this is a call to death or the imagined comfort of falling asleep in the Lord as the songs of my young years would have it, Patrick was saying on the phone when he called me, out of the blue—as the beloved cliché would have it—while I was sitting at my window in the Gadsden, looking north as the mountains disappeared behind the incoming fog. Were you saying the actor who plays Doc Holliday in the re-creation in the Gunfight of the OK Corral was saying, the mines here about, go right down into hell and that is why people come to Tombstone?

Only George understood, Karri came back in. He would have none of this sort of doodling. My patients talk like that, you remember, Thomas?, as if they are clearing their throats—minutes tick away then the hour or fifty minutes is up and we have had one or two sentences that mean anything... as when you, George, called saying you were not feeling well... not feeling well, I don't know what is the real matter—though he did know what was the real matter—they are giving me a poison so I can live to deal with the effects of the poison: is that what they call living today? Can you answer me that? Of course you can't—and I can't—and no one can...

You must not avoid, Karri says again, even if George has not but you think he is saying it again and again: as in Bulgaria no one can explain anything and if you try to explain anything to someone you know you sound crazy and if you are speaking you are crazy so you don't speak so you are crazy like everyone else. Inside me a piece of pig, do you know what that means: to carry inside you a piece of pig and your life depends on that piece of pig.

George never took himself in memory back to the countryside in Bulgaria... most Bulgarians are one two in rare cases only three or four generations from the soil... they speak a different language there or no language you can understand once you have left or thought to have left so it doesn't matter if you don't speak Bulgarian when you go to a village.

Remember you wrote to me, George said and Karri reminded me of it: In the winter after my father had died I had gone to the far country in Bulgaria, far from Sofia and was taken to visit Lydia's uncle who was taking care of her grandmother, who had one tooth left in her head: I took a little walk with this man, this gentle man, Gosho—Lydia called him, he was considered un-lucky, deeply unlucky because he had a heart condition and wasn't allowed to marry: he is the meaning of nema kizmet—no luck—in the town ever so briefly and a pig had been killed in the yard of a house nearby, hoisted up and the amount of blood, a sack of blood, saved in barrels for the long winter: every bit of the pig saved as it had had been tended for all those years as almost a family member, a member of the family you could say until the time, the time came for the man with the knife and the rope: the up ending...

And George supplied you with a commentary: in an American hospital they don't end you up but tell you to hop up on the table and lie down... but you never get over the thought of his hands inside your chest, really inside you—it's bad enough when a stranger touches you on the shoulder but why should you always think of Bulgaria?

Why should you get it all so right? And you do not go back among the Bulgarians because you well know no one would listen since you are not Bulgarian and while they don't listen to Bulgarians…

In that village I went along and saw *The French Connection* with maybe five or six people in the big auditorium in the kultur palas in the late afternoon… a certain number of shows and Lydia's uncle said most times they ran the movies in that place, day after day and no one went since most of the movies were Russian, but that did not matter… the strangeness of being met at the station with a cart and horse and the boy flicking his whip to get the mule going and Medy saying, he won a prize to go to Moscow, and he is not happy, no one would be happy with such a prize, but they gave out such prizes only in the countryside. They could not do it in Sofia but even here they knew that it was not a prize to go to Moscow for a week (second prize Gosho nudged Medy was two weeks in Moscow).

A horse drawn cart and Popeye Doyle… walking home from the *tri guyama studeno mastika* I fell into a ditch and was helped to the house… they would dare not hurt you a foreigner…

The local colour, enough of that, please, Karri is saying. Remember George found himself again living among Bulgarians when sometimes we talked. For a while when he was first in The United States of America he entertained the possibility he would not be living among these people. He refused to push his thought to saying: he wanted to be free of the Bulgarians.

He had enough of the Bulgarians.

What was it?—forty years—wasn't that long enough?

My father's only connection to Ireland was his last name and a green tie on St. Patrick's Day, you'd tell him, he told me. A fortunate man, he thought you, George would say. I scraped some of the Bulgarian off my name and there are no holidays at least in the New York and maybe nowhere in The United States of America that walk people up and down avenues celebrating what didn't want you in the first place. He never told anyone, as far as I know, he was always a little jealous of Lydia who had, once her mother was finally dead, successfully flown the Bulgarians. How fortunate she was.

Karri suggests I should distance what comes next. George often talked with you about the accident that brought you together. Vera was desperate enough one day, George would say, and asked Medy—that crazy woman, he would always add whenever her name was mentioned—to look after their children when they were very young. For a few weeks there were no problems but then Medy fell in the bathroom—you remember how fat she was and how small our bathroom was—and decided she had gotten shingles from the fall and then she—Medy, *Baba Roosha*, that crazy woman—decided the upstairs neighbors were trying to get her, wanting to hurt her in some way. Medy would show them. She ran the hot water in the bath tub all the time, day after day, night after night. This burnt out the hot water heater and wrecked the boiler, George said. Luckily we did not live in that building... but Vera's sister lived there... and Medy, that crazy woman, tied her to Vera, to the neighbors upstairs who did things all night...

Medy stabbed Vera's brother-in-law with a pen knife. I don't know all the circumstances. No one could ever tell me exactly what happened. It is like reading three newspapers about some little event.

The cops were called by someone who thought he had seen something but my brother-in-law didn't press charges, George said. The cops don't have time for people speaking languages they don't understand and my brother-in-law didn't want to get into trouble with the police and what came with the police knowing who you are and they knew Medy, that crazy woman, wasn't all right in the head. They had their own problems—and those problems edged into George's life in the sense, as he told me, he had to give thought to these people—my wife's sister and her husband the truck mechanic—these people who could not read, who could not listen, who could not look but who wanted, yes, wanted and wanted everything, the everything to be had with credit cards that, as they said, the stupid Americans just give you, so why shouldn't they want everything if the stupid Americans want you to have everything because this is what America teaches people like my relatives by marriage.

You should know about such people… don't you? George would say more as a hope he was not alone in his isolation midst these people, his relatives by marriage, who tip-toed around him because they look at me as if I am some sort of witch doctor—it is hard to believe such people exist still in New York City but not if you live in Brooklyn then and even now where they have human sacrifices in bathtubs and some of them are always cutting off pieces from young girls' bodies and making fires in corners of parks and saying strange words into the smoke: am I not right?

But your relatives don't do things like that…

How do you know? Just because they have white skin doesn't mean they don't think like that. They tip-toe around me because I work with the mind—they are so superstitious—and I know, always their question will begin: I had a dream last night… I tell them buy the book they sell in the bodega and make your fortune like all the other poor people making fortunes on their dreams—so many poor people with dreams to make them rich—though I do know and you know from the time you went to Melinda's mother's house that out in Southampton and other places like it you have rich people who also want to make money from their dreams or find new ways to not grow old or not to have children who will hate them or to path their lives into gardens filled with these beautiful flowers that come from talking to their psychics or rubbing their stones, or shining their auras or charting stars or shoving something up their rectums…

That's all they can say for themselves, Lydia would say.

Then YOU, GEORGE, called saying you were not feeling well… not feeling well, I don't know what is the real matter—though you did know what was the real matter—they are giving you a poison so you can live to deal with the effects of the poison: is that what they call living today? Can you answer me that—of course you can't—and you can't—and no one can—as when in Bulgaria no one can explain anything and if you try to explain anything to someone you know you sounded crazy and if you are speaking you are crazy so you don't speak so you are as crazy as everyone else because both silence and speaking are acts of crazy people in Bulgaria.

Inside me a piece of pig, do you know what it means: to carry inside you a piece of pig and your life depends on a piece of pig.

Next to Vera's sister or was it across the hall?—George finally lost interest in keeping track of these people, but you kept on and never stopped talking about when Lydia took you to meet a woman, up there in a darkness so thick— how hard it is to describe—a darkness ever present on the brightest summer day when you did visit this woman and it wasn't that the blinds or drapes were drawn… another sort of darkness, Lydia said, and I could not disagree with her: this woman who had once been a beauty, was said to have been a prostitute in Sofia and then in Argentina with a man who had a ranch the size of a state in the United States but now lived in that building mostly lying on bed with the drapes closed. Her face was full of wrinkles as deep as the ocean which Lydia said was a line from a famous Bulgarian poem by Yavarov…

I don't care for that woman, George would say. Every street in Pleven had women like that. Don't think I am being disagreeable. Every shadow has a woman with a story to tell you. That is where it always goes wrong. You listen to the story. Think you have discovered the secret of the human condition and what do you do with it?

Of course, Lydia had memories of Bulgaria, after all she was human, carrying even into America one book of poetry by this Yavarov, one of the scant few in Bulgaria to die from love, imagine, even in Bulgaria poets can die from love and having been sad their whole lives... and had left Bulgaria when she was eighteen, but maybe too tired after the being plunged into America, really plunged into Northern Wisconsin just in time for the clamp down of winter and the sure hand of the American's mother who knew what was best and did not argue at all about any of it.

But I am thinking, I told Karri as George had no interest, of another Lydia who did not know what a house dress was and my mother had been able to show her what it was and find her a comfortable one to wear. Such a garment was not known in Bulgaria and George who had heard this story changed the subject as he was want to do: Bulgarians don't have such an idea... it is something like their inability to express anger because the Bulgarian language is impoverished when to comes to gradations of feeling. In English you can fall through bothered, annoyed, pissed off, angered and end up in rage. In Bulgarian you went directly from irritation to rage. Bystanders beware.

George had worked his way from Bulgarian to German

to English becoming an amateur of such things and well knowing talk about language was a real and genuine way of putting people to sleep. Or it just shut them up because Americans in particular had no sense of grammar and were always afraid, really once the proverbial cat was out of the—bag, that a person was actually listening to how you spoke, the decent and prompt reply was to just shut up and say you had to be going…

With Bulgarians it was simple. You put food on the table. Made sure everyone had something to drink and smoke. You said hello, they said hello and you began to eat and drink and smoke. If you were lucky, nothing was said and people went home, again, another visit done with

Only George could have understood
Only George might have understood
If only George
Of course George
And while George
Did it ever happen?
Could George have known?

6 April 2021

Thomas McGonigle was born at 110 Willoughby Avenue, Brooklyn, some years ago. His patriotism is divided between: Patchogue, Dublin, Sofia and a base on East First Street in Manhattan. His published works include, *In Patchogue, The Corpse Dream of N. Petkov* (in English and Bulgarian), *Going to Patchogue, Diptych Before Dying* (in Bulgarian), *St. Patrick's Day: Another Day in Dublin*. Reviews and articles by Thomas McGonigle can be read at The Guardian (London), The Washington Post, Chicago Tribune, The Los Angeles Times, Newsday, The Hollins Critic.

abcofreading.blogspot.com

* 9 7 8 1 9 5 6 0 0 5 5 5 4 *